Mystery at the Red House

by Cornelia Meigs

Master Simon's Garden
Willow Whistle
The Wonderful Locomotive
The Covered Bridge
The Mounted Messenger
The Two Arrows
The Vanished Island
Wind in the Chimney
The Dutch Colt
Fair Wind to Virginia
Wild Geese Flying
Mystery at the Red House

Mystery at the Red House

by Cornelia Meigs

illustrated by Robert MacLean

The Macmillan Company
New York

A shortened version of *Mystery at the Red House* appeared in *Trails for Juniors* of the Methodist Publications, July, 1961.

Library of Congress catalog card number: 61–12354

FOURTH PRINTING, 1963

The Macmillan Company, New York
Brett-Macmillan Ltd., Galt, Ontario

Printed in the United States of America

For my namesake
Cornelia Whittemore Fales

CONTENTS

1

Treasure in the Well

Every house that has a happy family living in it has its own story, the story of how they first saw it, decided that they would like to live in it, found that it would be possible and settled down, but not always easily or without things happening. This, then, is the story of the Red House on the Clark's Hill Road, and of how, without exactly expecting to, the Grahams went to live there.

It was a June day when they first saw it. They were traveling north, and, late in the morning, were going up a long hill and beginning to feel that they had come very far. They had eaten early breakfast in the bare city apartment, with nearly all their furniture packed and sent to storage. Nina, sitting now in the front seat of the car with her father and mother on each side, heard her younger brother Jeff say behind them, "Arthur, you're taking up an awful lot of room. Move over can't you?"

Arthur was his springer spaniel, his very own dog whom he loved so much that he almost never spoke crossly to him. Nina knew that he must be getting very tired. Her father, Robert Graham, turned where a small road branched off and ran more steeply uphill than the way they had come. He drew a sigh as though he were getting tired too and stopped the car. "Won't this place do?" he asked hopefully. "If we have as hard a time finding a place to live as just deciding where to have a picnic along the way, we'll have a long journey to go."

The children's mother, Jane Graham, answered quickly, "Surely we can find a place to stop with more view. Just give us one more mile, past another turn and up this hill." Robert Graham agreed cheerfully and started the engine again. The car moved into the narrower road that wound upward before them. A little sign that they passed said "Clark's Hill."

They were changing their place of living, which is not easy to do. The apartment house in the city near the big Highgate University where Dr. Graham was a professor of history, was to be torn down. It was hard to find another place that would hold four people comfortably, especially people who could not afford a very great deal of rent. But this year the children's father did not have to teach, he was to have time off to write a book. After they had looked at a good many places, Jane Graham said suddenly one day:

"We've talked for years, the way all city people do, about moving to the country. Now is the time when we really can try it." So their furniture was packed away, the trunk of the car was filled with Professor Graham's notes and books and they had set out northward toward New England, to find a a house and a neighborhood where they could all be happy. But they had not seen anything that looked in the least hopeful yet, not even a place to sit down by the road and eat a midday dinner.

The car climbed on and the wide green country spread out below them, with the distant hills showing bigger and bigger until they were mountains. "Now," said Robert Graham as he stopped the car again, "Here's your mile."

They all exclaimed together, for they had come, as far as the picnic was concerned, to the perfect place. Hastily they all tumbled out of the car and Mrs. Graham said with delight, "Nothing could be better."

Below them the valley swept in a great curve, showing a small river marked by willow trees, with a little village under the spur of the hill. It was a very small village, but complete with square houses, a white church spire and a building with a belfry which must be a school. They were all set out, like toys out of a box, around an open space which everyone who lived there must have called the village green. Where they had stopped there was a stone wall on each side of the road and a smooth field that sloped down toward the valley. In the middle of the field was a big maple tree with a round shadow about its foot. Surely just the place for a picnic! Arthur went leaping and scampering across the grass, his long ears streaming in the wind, with his owner Jeff running close behind.

"Suppose," said Jane Graham, "that, since it's only half past eleven o'clock, we have some sandwiches now and you children rest yourselves and stretch your legs a little. We've had a long drive since that early start; we may have another before we stop somewhere for the night."

The picnic basket was unpacked and carried down to the maple tree, then Nina and Jeff were only too glad to seize their sandwiches and race after Arthur. He had jumped over one stone wall into the road, and then over the one opposite where big trees grew close together on ground that went uphill.

"Don't go too far," their mother called after them. "We'll blow the car horn when your dinner is ready." The children gave an agreeing shout as

they went over the second wall and plunged into the thick bushes. But as they pressed forward they came first to open spaces among the trees, and then to a broad driveway that could not have been much used lately, for there was grass growing on it, and only a single line of wheel tracks up the middle. Above they could make out the shape of a very big house with broad chimneys and rows of tall windows that were all closed.

"There can't be anyone living there," Nina said, and so, when they came close, they felt that it was quite allowable to sit down on the wide steps that led up to the great front door. Even Arthur, with his tongue hanging out, was willing to wait for a little time beside them. They sat very quietly, looking down at the woods and fields below and Nina was wondering who could have lived there and gone away to leave so beautiful a place alone.

Arthur got restless first and went exploring with his nose along the big piazza. He began to paw at something below the door and Jeff got up to see what it was. "It's a piece of paper," he told Nina, "some kind of a message pushed so far in that you could hardly see it." He stooped to pull it out. It was indeed a folded paper which came open as he handed it to her. It must have been there for some time, since it was yellow with dampness, but the typewriting was still clear. She could see at a glance that it was not a letter, so that it seemed all right to read it. It was some kind of a verse.

"This is the first of the clues to follow:
Look for a man whose head is hollow,
With the battered-est hat you ever saw,
With big black boots and legs of straw."

She read it a second time, for it seemed like pure nonsense. Jeff took the paper and read it more slowly to himself. He was eight years old to Nina's eleven and reading did not go quite so quickly with him.

"It says at the top 'Clue number one,'" he said. "What's a clue?"

"It must be for a treasure hunt," Nina guessed. "Don't you remember how we went on one at Roddy Owen's birthday party, how we found a slip of paper that told us how to go on and look for another one, until the last one told us where the treasure was hidden? When we found it at last there was something in the package for everyone at the party."

"But whose treasure hunt is this?" Jeff persisted. "This paper has been here a long time. Why didn't anybody ever come to find it?"

Why indeed? Nina could not answer that, but she jumped up. "Let's look for the others," she said.

"A man whose head is hollow," was not a simple thing to find, but they started boldly out down the wide driveway, crossed the rough grass which had not been cut for weeks or months and turned toward an open place between the trees which brought them to a gate and a field. If the young corn that was growing in it had been a little higher, they would not have caught sight of the figure that stood alone in the middle, an awkward figure with stiff arms stretched out. It did not move as they came near. Though they had never seen one before, they knew at once that it was a scarecrow, put out to frighten away the birds that would have pulled up the sprouting corn. They walked to it, treading carefully between the corn rows.

Sure enough, the figure's head was a big tin can with a face painted on it and a very torn old hat pulled down over its top. Its coat and broken old boots were stuffed with straw. A stick had been pushed through the sleeves for arms, one end was split and a folded paper had been stuck into it. "He's holding it out to us," Jeff cried as he ran to take the message. It was yellower and more faded than the other one for it had been in the direct rain, and they had to go over and over the words until they got them all.

"Go uphill now, where the bright brook
turns,
Round the Island Rock, with its crown
of ferns;
There in the shade and the cool and
green
Another clue may perhaps be seen."

The noisy little brook was not hard to find, but they had to walk upstream some distance before they came to the place where it made a bend and flowed on each side of a great, gray rock. Stepping stones led them across to the great rock covered with moss and lichens and, at the top, with a bank of waving ferns. It was not easy to climb up the smooth sides, and it was only by each one's clambering up a little way and then helping the other that they both got to the top. They could see where the brook came plunging down from high up on the hillside, a regular mountain stream. They searched through the deep, bending ferns that stood around their knees and found the folded paper at last, between two stones. This held a longer verse than the others, but it had suffered more from the wind and rain, so that they could make out only the last few lines:

"... where the wind in the grass can
creep and run
And apples are gold in the summer
sun,
On the biggest branch, in the highest
cleft,
A message for you has been set and
left."

They were beginning to feel as though the messages had really been left for them, and they went racing down the bank of the stream to find where it ran out into an old orchard. In the middle, the biggest apple tree they had ever seen stood knee-deep in summer hay. They each stopped to sample a June apple among those which lay in the grass; the taste was like honey inside the pale yellow skin. They had to climb high to reach the forked branch; it seemed as though the message had been meant for someone taller than either of them. It told them:

"To the garden fence, I bid you go,
Where the yellow speckled lilies grow.
The way so far you have found and traced,
You are past half way, make haste, make
haste."

They had come far down the hill now, and the fields ended. Over to the right was a white fence and, yes, another house, low and painted dark red with white window frames, like many New England houses. Four oak trees with sweeping branches stood around it. The clump of tiger lilies next to the fence were only budding and were full of weeds, but here the message was stuck on a stake among their thick roots where it had been well sheltered from the rain. It was very short.

"You want to know the next step, then,
You'll have to ask of Mrs. Wren."

They had no need to hesitate now. Over at the house, under the eaves of the porch, was a small birdhouse with Mrs. Wren sitting on the perch by the door, sending out a stream of sound that was half singing and half scolding. The message was pushed under the edge of her roof. It was drier and easier to read than any of the others.

"Well, well, now you're tired and thirsty, I fear.
Are you hot? Did you run, when the prize was so near?
Did you press on in haste? Well, be of good cheer,
Just a dozen yards more and the treasure is HERE!"

"Here?" echoed Nina as she read it aloud. "I

don't see any place where it could be, not any place at all."

They went up on the long porch of the red house and looked carefully around. The doors were all locked, but they could peer in at the windows. "What a sweet house," Nina said, "What a dear house." And after a little time she said, "It's just about the size of a house that we've been looking for." There was a big stone fireplace in the living room, and a broad couch and comfortable chairs around it. Jeff, who was very observant said thoughtfully, "That couch cover looks as though people were allowed to put their feet on it."

They went peering and peeping, but nowhere did they find a sign of anything that might lead them those last few yards to the treasure. Arthur had trotted at their heels for all of the way, and now went snuffing across the grass, rough and uncut like the lawn above.

"What's that, over there, where Arthur is?" Jeff asked.

Nina was rather proud that she knew, she had seen one when she was visiting her grandmother. "It's a well," she said. It had a high stone curb around it to save people from falling into it, with a wooden roof across the top to keep dirt and leaves from dropping in. They walked toward it and saw that the cover opened on a hinge. Nina had the last paper in her hand and was rereading it. "Well, well, now you're tired—"

"Oh, oh," she cried out. "It says 'well, well' and at the end it says 'well' again. It must mean that the treasure is in the well." She flung up the wooden cover and the two hung over the edge. They could see the glimmer of water far below and that the big wooden bucket hung halfway down. "I'm going to bring it up," she said, and took hold of the handle that wound up the rope.

The bucket squeaked and groaned and came slowly up, nearer and nearer.

"There's something in it," shouted Jeff. "Something white." They brought the bucket up to the very top and reached in to lift out a heavy square package, wrapped in white paper and not only tied but sealed with red wax. It was just then that they heard the sound of their car horn from the road below. It was nearer than they would have guessed.

"We won't open it," Nina said. "We'll just show it to them first the way it is." They came out into the driveway of the red house and saw that it was the same one that wound up to the big house above. It went out to the road through a gap in the wall, not very far uphill from where their car was parked.

They rushed down to their father and mother, waiting in the field below. Their explanations came with a rush and were not very clear. "There was a treasure hunt, but nobody came—the clue said look in the well—we pulled up the bucket—" They handed their package to their father and he put it in the middle of the picnic tablecloth. "We'll each have a guess as to what is in it," he said. They sat down to eat, and each guessed.

Jeff thought it might be a toy train but they told him it was not large and heavy enough. Mrs. Graham thought it might be a very big box of candy. Robert Graham thought it might be a very fine set of chessmen. Nina's turn came last.

"I don't care very much what is in it," she said. "Only that it must be a great surprise."

"Nina was really the one who found it," her mother declared. "So she ought to open it."

Nina hesitated for a minute, then reached across to take up the package. Dampness had weakened the paper, so that when she picked it up it split apart on all sides and half a dozen little leather boxes came tumbling out. One of them hit the edge of a plate and fell open. Out of it came a sudden ray of brilliant green that was almost blinding. They looked at one another in wonder and, one after the other, they opened the rest. Blue, red, gleaming white, they came pouring out, a heap of jewels, glinting and glittering in the middle of the old picnic tablecloth.

"Are they—are they real?" Nina gasped and her father answered. His voice was not excited, like hers, only grim.

"Sure they're real. And they're worth a fortune! What on earth are we to do with them?"

2

A Message

Two years before, the family had been able to make a quick trip to England where Professor Graham had been asked to lecture. Though the two children were younger then, they never forgot anything that they saw there. Nina remembered especially the Tower of London and the English Crown Jewels in their great round glass case, watched over by the Tower Guards. The crowns, the scepter, the Sword of State, and the other signs of British royalty were all there, set with glittering emeralds, rubies, and diamonds which, with their magic beauty, gave Nina a quiver inside as she looked at them. The jewels that she saw now, piled up before her on the tablecloth, gave her the same tingling excitement. They were fewer and smaller, but some were almost equal in size and brilliance to those she had seen in the Tower. But here there were no Tower Guards. Certainly the first thing to do was to get them back into their boxes again. Jeff was looking anxiously over his shoulder as though someone already might be coming to try to steal them.

The leather boxes had names fastened to them, but they were nicknames which meant nothing to strangers, "Toots, Highlo, and Budge," with two boxes and sometimes three for each one. The split torn paper gave no clue as to the owner, even the seals were only red blots of wax to hold it firm. As fast as the boxes were filled again, Robert Graham put them into his pockets. It took all he had to hold them.

"I'm not going to be responsible for them a minute longer than I have to," he declared. "We'll go down to the village at once to put them into a bank for safekeeping or to turn them over to the police. I'll try the bank first, and we must hurry or it will be closed."

Mrs. Graham and Jeff—and Arthur, decided that they would stay there and get the picnic things together and take a little walk. Nina and her father got into the car to drive down to the little town that they had seen from above. It was such a small village that they thought at first that they might not find a bank, but there was one, fronting on the village green, opposite the church. They went in and Robert Graham said to the young man behind the window, "I would like to rent a safety deposit box here to—to put some valuables in."

The young man hesitated a minute and looked doubtful. "You're a stranger in town Mr. —?"

"Graham," he was told. "Mr. Graham. You're going to be here some time?"

"No," Nina's father said, rather unwisely. "I'm just passing through."

"And you want to leave valuables behind?" The bank man looked more doubtful still. "We don't, as a rule, do business with people we don't know, sir. Could you give us some names to write to, so that we can ask a few necessary questions. Or do you know anyone here in Durham?"

"No," Robert Graham admitted. "I don't have any acquaintance here. But I'm a perfectly respectable professor of history in a famous university. I could give you a dozen names of people there who could tell you all about me. But I am in something of a hurry, so perhaps you would let me see the bank's president and let him decide."

"It just happens that I am the president," the young man answered modestly. "We have a very small force and when the others are out for lunch I help out at the window. And I have to say that we cannot accept your application for a safety deposit box. Banks in the country have their own worries and more than once it has happened that people want to leave valuables behind that do not—exactly—belong to them. So we have to make a hard and fast rule."

"Very well then, I will bid you good afternoon," Professor Graham said in his grandest manner. He walked out with Nina following at his heels.

"What a hateful man," she said as she came up beside him. "What a wicked, horrid man!"

Her father walked a little way along the edge of the green without saying anything, and then he burst out laughing. "People want to leave valuables behind that don't belong to them," he repeated what the bank president had said. "It's just what I was trying to do, although the difference is that I intend to find the owner, as soon as I have the miserable jewels in safekeeping. Well, if the bank will have none of us, we'll have to try the police."

It was harder to find a policeman in Durham than it had been to find a bank. "Oh, it's Clem Matherson you want," one person said when they asked him. "I'm not sure that he's in town today." Another man "thought I saw Clem maybe two hours ago," but had no idea where he might be now. At last they found his little headquarters office on the narrow street that led off the green. It was a single room with a battered desk and an old coat hanging on a peg. They went in to wait. Nina sat on a stool by the window and saw, very soon, that they were in luck and that he was coming, for a shabby little car drew up outside and Officer Matherson came in.

He was a tall man with wrinkles in his forehead and with such a kindly, honest face that Robert Graham seemed to feel at once that they could tell him the whole story. He explained everything. "My daughter and son found these," he ended, drew out the leather boxes and opened them. Nina watched the man closely. How surprised would the man be and what would he think? But his steady New England face did not change, he looked the jewels over as though he handled such things every day, made a little note on a paper and said quietly, "You'd better put them up now. We don't want anyone happening to come in and seeing them." The story that Nina and Jeff found them in the well did not seem to surprise him at all—he evidently had no doubts about its truth. Nina began to help put them back into their boxes while her father said, "But I wanted to leave them with you."

The policeman shook his head. "I'd like to help you out and take them but I have no authority for anything as valuable as this. I could write to my superior officer over at Hampton—that's the nearest big town—and you might be able to take it up with him."

"Couldn't you telephone?" Professor Graham

asked, but once more the big man shook his head.

"Telephones in this town aren't very private; the telephone girl might talk. I'd hate to have it get around that anything like this had been found. And if you would advertise to try to find the owner, any crook within five hundred miles would be after you to claim them and have some smart story to prove they were his. All you can do, sir, is to keep them as safe as you can until we manage to find who they belong to. I'll ask what questions I can and get my boss to do the same. It stands to reason that nobody would leave a fortune in a well bucket and not care what becomes of it."

There was nothing that they could do but take the boxes and stow them in Robert Graham's pockets again. "I wish—" Nina was saying as they drove away. She was going to say that she wished she had not found them, but it was not true. Here was a true adventure and there was no telling how it might turn out. She knew that her father was thinking deeply, and that he was greatly puzzled.

"But we can't go on and take them with us," he burst out at last. "And if I can't leave them with anybody how can we go on anyway? And we haven't anywhere to live. We can't go to a motel laden down with some other person's fortune in jewels." The last thing came out finally, the most worrying of all. "And I have my book to write."

They came up the hill and stopped in the road opposite to where they had set out their picnic lunch. Mrs. Graham and Jeff were not to be seen.

"I think I know where they are," Nina said, "Just go a little farther up the road."

They reached the gap in the wall where the driveway came out and turned in. There was the small red house under the dipping branches of the big oaks, and Jane Graham and Jeff, with Arthur, were on the porch. The top of the well was still open and Nina went across the grass to close it. No, she was not sorry that they had followed the clues leading to the treasure—there was too much that might come of it. Her mother was just coming down the steps. "I thought that this house—" they both began together and stopped.

"Jeff and Arthur showed me this place," Jane Graham said. "Just the right size for us and with such a view. But it's not for us." She pointed to a small sign, outside the porch railing, that Nina and Jeff had overlooked. It said, very surprisingly, something that no such sign had ever said before:

"This house is not for rent."

Robert Graham stood looking at it for a long minute. "The owner might perhaps change his mind," he suggested. "Although if he's the kind of man who leaves jewels in the well, there's no guessing what he will or will not do. I have no doubt that so many people who went by on the road stopped to ask if they could rent it that he got tired of telling them they couldn't. But the place looks as though it had been empty for a good while, months certainly." It was true; the grass and bushes had all grown tall and the flowers were struggling through a mass of weeds.

"We could be happy in this house," Nina's mother was beginning when she was interrupted by a shout from Jeff. He had gone round to the back where none of them had come, so far. "Oh see what's here," he was calling.

They all came in haste. Across the back was a row of windows, closed with shutters now, but one of them had blown open. When they came to look in they saw that inside was a very long room that stretched behind the living room and the kitchen. There were rows of bookshelves all along the walls which showed that it was a library. But a second glance made one think, no, it was a dining room.

A long table stood in the middle of the room with chairs drawn up to it. The table was covered with a white cloth and was elaborately set out. Nina almost whispered as she said. "It was a feast! The feast that went with the treasure hunt. And it was someone's birthday."

In the middle was a very big cake with candles and with tall candlesticks on each side of it. There were vases for flowers, but there was nothing left in them but dried stems and leaves. Places were set for six and there were favors by each plate, little exquisite glass animals and the snapping crackers that hold paper caps. There were cards leaning up against the glasses, most certainly with names on

them. Nina could guess that three of the names were Highlo, Budge, and Toots. Jeff said, "See, someone even lighted the candles in the candlesticks and they're all burned out. But they didn't light the candles on the cake."

Who had been invited there, whose were the places, who was to have sat at the head of the table? Yet it was true, here was the feast to follow the treasure hunt, and the people who were to have found the treasure, to have received the almost priceless gifts, had never come. What could it all mean?

"I, for one, can't even guess at what it's all about," Robert Graham said as he turned away. "The afternoon is getting on and we have to find ourselves somewhere to sleep before it gets too dark. We don't want to go too far; we have to make an effort tomorrow to find out, somehow, who it is that owns these jewels that have so inconveniently fastened themselves upon us. Well, we must move along."

They all went back to where the picnic had been held and gathered up the last things. "Here," Robert Graham said, "I'm tired of being a walking treasury. Find something to put these into, won't you, Jane? They'll travel just as well in a basket as in my bulging pockets."

The children's mother found an empty brown paper bag, and, as Professor Graham emptied his pockets she put the leather boxes into it, all wrapped together in the last of the paper napkins. She twisted the top of it and put it into the bottom of the picnic basket. Robert Graham picked it up and carried it up the hill. Jeff had not been of very much help in the last packing up; he had kept running off after Arthur and they both had to be called back. But now they were ready.

"Not a single car has gone by since we stopped here," Jane Graham said. "I do wish someone had passed who could have told us the best place to spend the night."

But someone was about to go by, someone very small indeed, who did not, at the first glance, look as though he would be of much help to them. Robert Graham had just got over the wall to the car, and the others were following, when a little boy came trotting out of the driveway above and came down toward them. He had as companion a long-legged awkward puppy who, being a police dog, was already well above ordinary dog size. The little boy could not have been more than five years old. He kept saying "Stop Casey, wait Casey," as the dog galloped ahead of him. In spite of the fact that he was coming as fast as his short legs would bring him, he was carrying something very carefully. He came close and they could see that he had reddish hair, a round face and very round blue eyes. He handed what he was carrying to Professor Graham and, of all the surprises of this remarkable day, this was the most unexpected. It was an egg.

"Thank you, son," said Robert Graham gravely. "But what is it for?"

The little boy could not talk very well, especially when he was in a hurry. "It's f-for you," he said. "R-read it."

Robert Graham turned it over in his hand. It was true that there was something written on it, scrawled in black letters. It said: "Help. Come quickly."

3

The Red House

Robert Graham was not a person to stop and ask questions when he got a message asking for help, even though it was written on an egg. "Can we get there in the car? Then jump in," he said, "and show me the way. Is it up in that direction?" He waved his hand toward the grass-grown driveway. The little boy had nodded vigorously and now climbed in beside him. Mrs. Graham, Nina, Jeff, and Arthur had crowded into the back seat. They had put the picnic things into the trunk, shut it with a slam, and locked it.

They went up the curving driveway, past the

great square brick house with its four huge chimneys, turned round a half circle in front of it and went past the barns and garages. The little boy had told them his name, "C-Clyde," and waved his hand vaguely toward the road to show them where he lived. He pointed now and they went past the biggest barn to a smaller building behind it. The door was gaping open and windows were open above. "There?" Robert Graham asked. Clyde said "Yes" and jumped out of the car almost before it had stopped. They all followed.

The place had evidently been built for a hay barn once, but it had a second floor now, and the lower part had been fitted up as a carpenter shop, with a bench along one wall and all the necessities of a shop in the corners. At the back was a steep flight of narrow stairs and Clyde said, "Up there." Robert Graham raised his voice, "Is anybody here?"

A muffled sound from above could be taken as someone answering "Yes."

They went up in procession, following Clyde, with the two dogs last. This upper space was a long room which now had even less to do with barns than the shop below, though a big pulley in the ceiling showed where once a rope and pulley had brought up bales of hay. There were shelves all along the walls covered with bottles and jars, with strange-shaped bowls and jugs, with scales for weighing and glasses for measuring. The children had been often enough to their father's office at the university, and had gone from there to visit friends of his and theirs in the science building next door, so that they knew a laboratory when they saw one. "A place where professors work with things that mostly smell queer," was the way Jeff defined a laboratory, but to Nina it was a wonderful spot where any kind of odd thing could happen.

But they did not look much now at what might be on the shelves or spilling out of the half-unpacked boxes scattered about the room. There was a long beam lying slantwise across the floor, having evidently crashed down from the roof, and someone was lying, face downward, pinned under its weight. Nina got to him first and stooped over. "Are you very badly hurt?" she asked anxiously.

"No, not to signify." The answer was not very distinct, for the man's face was pressed close against the floor. The beam was lying across his shoulders so that he could scarcely turn his head or move his arms. "The beam caught against a block there, so it didn't crush me flat, but it is slipping a little and it may come down with its full weight any minute. There's a ladder and a rope down in the shop. If you could get it up over that pulley—" He had spoken haltingly, but managed to make himself understood. Certainly there was not a second to spare. They all went plunging down the stairs to fetch the rope and the ladder, except Nina. Her mother had been trying to tuck a handkerchief

between the man's face and the splintery floor. Nina knelt down to finish slipping it in.

"I'm so very sorry," she said. The words certainly did not sound like enough, but it was all that she could think of to say. He managed to move his head a very little and she got the handkerchief under his cheek.

"Thank you," he said, speaking a little more clearly. "That's the first breath I've drawn that wasn't full of dust from the floor." She stood looking down at him, wondering what else she could do. Suddenly a very unexpected sound came out of a dark corner. "Cluck," it went, very loud and firm. "Cluck."

Clyde had come up the steps and went over toward the sound. "There, there," he said soothingly. The young man explained, though his words still came out slowly.

"It's Clyde's good friend Sally Hen, and luckily for me he comes up here every day to pay her a visit. She's stolen her nest and is sitting on eggs up here, in a box that had some straw in it, instead of down in his grandmother's henhouse as she should. If it hadn't been for that, Heaven knows how long I'd have been lying here, waiting for the beam to drop the rest of the way. I heard your voices down the hill and thought you must be people having a picnic. Clyde is pretty little to carry much of a message, and he couldn't find any paper for me to write on. But he went and got an egg from under Sally

Hen, it was very brave of him because she didn't like it a bit. He found a pencil I was marking boxes with and he held the egg where I could manage to write on it. I told him not to try to run too fast or he would break it. Clyde's a good fellow."

By this time the rope had been carried up and the ladder had been brought and placed against the slanting roof. Robert Graham went up it with Jeff at his heels, since Jeff was a perfect cat on ladders in the gymnasium. Together they got the rope over the pulley. The two came down to tie one end of the rope around the beam that had pinned the man to the floor, and to stretch out the other end so that they could all get hold of it.

"Now," said the children's father, "all of you be ready. I'll count and when I get to three, all of you pull with everything that's in you, and keep pulling until I get to ten. Give it your best. One—two—"

Numbers of people can count for something even if some of them are not very large. Nina was nearest her father and mother, then came Jeff, then Clyde. "Three," Robert Graham said, and they all pulled together, panting with effort. "Four—five—" The big beam creaked, shifted a little, then moved and lifted and the man under it doubled up and rolled quickly out of the way. He did not get clear a second too soon, for by the time the counting got to nine the rope gave a loud crack and snapped and the beam fell with a crash that shook the whole building. The young man—it showed now that he was a very young man indeed—sat up and was running his hands through his yellow rumpled hair to get the dirt and splinters out of it. The hen came out of her corner, screaming as only frightened hens can scream. Clyde took her in his arms to comfort her.

"That was a close thing," observed the young man cheerily. He got stiffly to his feet while they crowded about him to know how much he was hurt. "Just bruised, I think," he told them as he tried moving one arm and then another and putting his shoulders back. "No, I believe that's all the damage."

A dozen questions asked him how the thing had happened. "I saw yesterday, when I came, that one of the rafters was cracked; it must have been one of the big storms last winter that did it. I was foolish enough not to wait for someone to come who knew how to repair it. I climbed up by myself to see what the damage was and down it came, taking me with it. Am I right in thinking that you people were having a picnic down near the red house by the gate? I'm surely grateful to you, whatever brought you there."

They did some explaining on their part and he, in his turn, told them something about himself, "which isn't much," he declared. His name, it seemed, was Kent Clark and he had just finished his first year at Highgate University, the same university as Professor Graham's. It was very large and was the most famous one in seven states. "I'm studying to be a chemist," he said. "I have wanted to be one ever since my Cousin Charley let me putter around this laboratory where he did his own experiments, and gave me my first chemistry set when I was nine." His professor, so he told them, had given him a problem to work out during the vacation. "It's a piece of a very big thing of his own and he didn't have time to go over all the possible experiments, himself."

The owners of this whole estate, Kent said, were his cousins. He knew that they were all away, but he was certain the laboratory was not being used so he was taking it over for the summer. "Just as long as I don't blow it up or set it on fire, nobody will mind. And then, because I was here, the man in the village who was left in charge of the place when the family was away, wanted to go away himself, so he turned the responsibility over to me, most certainly without my wanting it. He just brought up the keys and the papers and left them with me and that was all."

It was Jeff who blurted out the question that they all wanted to ask. "Why does it say down there at the red house that it isn't for rent?"

"Oh, my Cousin Charles said that people were always stopping and saying 'What a cute place. Could we rent it for the summer?' even when they could see that he lived there and they ought to know that it wasn't to be rented." Kent himself, he explained, slept in the little apartment at the back of this building that had been the chauffeur's quarters. "But there's nobody around now, nobody at all," he ended. His voice dropped as though there was something about their all being away that troubled him.

Nina's father got up from the stool where he had been sitting to listen. "We have to go on," he said. "Perhaps you can tell us the best place to spend the night. We can camp out, but I hardly believe this is going to be the sort of night for it."

"You could camp out in the Red House itself," Kent answered quickly. "Mrs. Gregory, that's Clyde's grandmother, comes down every few days to air it and sweep it. I have the right to give you permission because, as I said, willy-nilly I have charge of the estate."

It seemed much too pleasant an invitation to resist, so that in the end Robert Graham took the keys, saying, "Just for one night," and they all turned to go down the narrow stairs.

"Are you certain that you are all right?" Nina's mother asked as they were leaving and he laughed and said, "Sure I am. I expect to do a good evening's work here in the laboratory before I sleep. And I'll get a carpenter up tomorrow to get this beam up again. If you have Clyde take home a note to his grandmother, she'll send him down in the morning with some milk and eggs for your breakfast. And I would like to try to thank you—"

"Don't say anything about that," Robert Graham interrupted him firmly. "Who wouldn't come in answer to a message on an egg? And you are giving us a night's lodging."

"Not very much of one, I fear," Clark returned. "You'll find some candles in the kitchen cupboard, I think. Everything is turned off. You will have to get water out of the well though it hasn't been used for a long time. Do you know where it is, over there toward the white fence?" Yes, they knew where it was.

The others were carrying down the ladder and Nina was last with the coil of rope. She opened her mouth to tell him what they had found in the well; then she recollected that her father and mother seemed to have thought it wiser not to speak of it, so probably she should not either, until they knew Kent better. But she looked over her shoulder to say good night, and he answered with such a friendly smile, "Good night, Nina." It really seemed as though they might get to be good friends, particularly because she liked laboratories so much. But no, tomorrow they would be going on, for they still had to find a place to live.

It was quite true that the small, neat red house was fully ready for anyone to come into it; Clyde's grandmother had kept it shining. They made a fire in the fireplace and heated soup for supper and other things out of cans, for they had a good supply to be ready for possible camping. They were tired with the long day of travel, but they were full of gay laughter as they did their rather awkward cooking and got together a bountiful meal. Then all of a sudden they were overcome with sleepiness and could hardly keep awake long enough to spread their blankets and arrange their pillows.

Nina fell asleep in almost no time at all, but she awoke late in the night and heard the wind in the trees and rain coming down on the roof. Her bedroom was downstairs, next to her father and mother's, while Jeff slept in a little gabled one above. Her door was partly open and through it she could see the red coals of the fire. How warm and dry and safe they were, with all the dark and wet outside. How wonderful that they were really sleeping in the little red house which she had wished they could live in, from the moment they first saw it. But there was that sign, outside, below her window, "This house is not for rent."

When she woke again it was broad daylight with the rain all cleared away, and a glorious summer day beginning. She could see mountains beyond the window and a great arch of brilliant blue sky. She thought she heard her mother walking about in the kitchen and she jumped up and dressed quickly for she liked to help with breakfast. And breakfast here, in the house which she felt that she had found, would be a very special occasion. There was an apron folded in the bottom of her suitcase and she slipped it on so that her mother would know at once that she had come out to help.

But when she came into the kitchen, her mother was not walking about, but was sitting by the table with her face bowed in her hands. She lifted her head and her face was desperate with worry.

"Nina," she said, "can you remember where we put the jewels?"

So much had happened, all at once, yesterday, and Nina had been so sound asleep, that for a moment she could not remember.

"I put them into a paper bag," her mother was saying, "the bag that had had the cold chicken in it, the one that was the strongest. And I pushed it into the very bottom of the basket and we put the basket into the trunk and locked it. I feel sure that I saw the bag again when we were getting things out for supper. I may even have set it on the kitchen table. But I was so tired and sleepy and was thinking so much about Kent Clark and how lucky it was that he was not badly hurt, that it drove such things as jewels out of my head. I may have gone to bed leaving the bag on the table, and I know we forgot to lock up. Do help me look for the jewels. I can hardly believe, even yet, that we really found them."

It was Nina who had found them, but she had never thought for a minute that her father and mother might not have put them away. The table was certainly empty now. The door to the little back porch stood open, the wind might have blown it back in the night, and it was swinging to and fro. On the back step there were three bottles of milk and a box of eggs. Clyde had evidently brought them down from his grandmother's as they had asked him to do. There was no use in looking all about the back porch, all about the kitchen again, all through the living room and the bedrooms. The only thing that was certain was that the jewels were gone.

4

The Dog Casey

Nina and her mother stood looking helplessly at each other. It was clear enough that the jewels had vanished, but by whose hand? A question was rising up in both their minds, but it was Nina who managed to get it partly into words first. "That little boy, Clyde. He was here early. Do you think—"

She could not really say it and her mother answered at once. "I do not believe it could possibly have been Clyde. I think I never saw a nicer little boy. But he might have seen somebody."

Jeff came running down the stairs, with Arthur at his heels. The spaniel ran to scratch at the front door, for dog instinct had evidently told him that there was another of his kind outside. "Didn't Clyde tell us that he and his grandmother lived just up the road?" Mrs. Graham said. "Run up there, Jeff, won't you, and ask if he saw anyone when he came with the eggs." Jeff opened the door and ran out after Arthur, leaving his mother and Nina to go over every inch of the kitchen and the living room again. But it was of no use, there was nothing to be found.

Jeff crossed the lawn of ragged grass and stopped at the gate. He saw Clyde coming toward him, pausing every few minutes to call "Casey, here Casey." When he came close Jeff saw that he was crying.

"Have you seen a d-dog," Clyde asked, stammering and sobbing at the same time. "Our dog Casey. He's lost."

"How long ago?" Jeff asked.

The little boy answered, "Oh, only just a little while ago. He f-followed me down to the Red House and he wouldn't come back because my granny had given him a smack. It was only a little one, but Casey's feelings get hurt easily."

"What was the smack for?" Jeff wished to know.

"For s-stealing bacon," Clyde returned, "the whole package. But Granny was sorry she s-smacked him and she s-said she would f-forgive him if he c-came home."

"I'll help you look for him," Jeff offered. It was

plain that Clyde could not answer any questions, not until his dog was found. They came back into the overgrown garden. "He might be looking for a place to bury the bacon," Jeff suggested, knowing about dogs and then asked, "Is he your very own dog or your grandmother's?"

No, Clyde told him, Casey used to belong at the Red House, "until everybody went away." Clyde, now that he had help at hand, had stopped his sobbing and they both went searching and peering among the thick shrubs and the trees whose branches swept to the ground. The flower beds were high with weeds, but in one there was a patch of bare earth and the paw mark of a dog, rather a large dog.

"That's Casey," Clyde shouted joyfully. It was the complete end of his tears. Very soon after they found the bacon in a mangled state, lying on the path that led to the kitchen door. They heard Arthur yelping in the bushes and wondered why Casey was not barking with him. A little farther away the grass was littered with bits of brown paper and in another moment the two dogs came into view, Casey with his head held high to carry a large brown-paper bag and Arthur following him in hot pursuit. Jeff ran after them as though he had wings on his feet, calling, "Arthur! Here Arthur!" but in a minute Arthur had snatched the bag from his awkward friend and was racing away with it. He lay down finally under a thick currant bush and began to chew in delight on the heavy brown paper.

"Catch him! Oh! catch him!" Jeff called to Clyde who was coming in on the dogs from another direction, but Arthur sprang up and made off again with the whole contents of the bag falling out and scattering in every direction.

Jeff set himself to pick up what had been spilled on the grass. Some of the little leather boxes had tooth marks on them, but none of them had broken open. Nina had come out of the house now and was following them, gathering up the boxes in her apron. She and Jeff counted them and found that they had them all. "The bag had chicken in it once," Jeff declared, not wishing it to seem as though Arthur had done anything more than any

dog might do, and that he and Casey were not really to be blamed. They left Clyde, joyfully reunited to his dog again, to go home carrying what was left of the bacon, and rushed into the house to announce, "We have them, we have them all." Jeff made haste to explain, "It was Arthur that got them away from Casey."

Their father had come in, still in his bathrobe, just in time to get their report. "We're a pretty family to have charge of someone else's collection of jewels," he remarked.

"We're just not used to having things like that around us," Jane Graham lamented. "I just can't keep thinking about them all the time and that someone might steal them."

"We might bury them," Jeff said helpfully. "But then we might forget where they were." His father was laying out the boxes on the table.

"I would like to drop them back into the well that they came out of," Professor Graham said. "But there must be a cupboard in the house with a lock on it, where they can stay until we leave later today."

They were just getting breakfast on the table when Kent Clark came in, looking brushed and tidier now, although his yellow hair would always look as though the wind had been blowing through it. He seemed not at all the worse for what had happened the afternoon before. "I wanted to make sure that you had been comfortable and had a good sleep," he said. He spoke a little shyly but he seemed truly interested in hearing that they had enjoyed their night in the Red House. They invited him to have breakfast with them and he sat down, though he was a little reluctant at first. But presently, as he sat between Nina and Jeff, he was talking and laughing as if they all were friends of long standing. His work in the laboratory up on the hill would, he told them, give him extra credit for the next college year and also, he hoped, bring him a scholarship. "I'm not sure that I can go back without a scholarship," he said. "And I have to go. I have to learn to be a chemist. I haven't ever wanted to be anything else, once I got old enough not to want to be a fireman."

They had finished breakfast but were still sitting around the table. The fresh mountain air was blowing in through the open windows, and the long grass in the garden was bowing in the wind. Kent Clark had something more to say, though he hesitated a little before beginning.

"I thought of it in the night," he told them. "You said you were looking for a house and were sorry this one was not for rent. As I told you, I have to take care of things here and among the instructions that were turned over to me was the plan to find a caretaker to live here in the Red House, a family that I knew about, who would see to the place properly. I do know you, Professor Graham, we're at the same university, even though among the thousands there you have never seen me. Dr. Craig, my chemistry professor, knows you and has talked about you. And if you wouldn't mind being called caretakers, and if you would really like to stay on—why it could be arranged."

There was quiet for a moment while they took in this large new idea. Nina broke it, without meaning to, by a little squeal of delight. Kent looked at her and smiled. "Nina accepts," he said. "How about the rest of you?"

They did not have to think very long. One look passed between the children's father and mother and they both nodded. "We accept, too," they said almost together. Nina let out a great sigh of happiness. Their house, their very own house! She had been sure from the minute she saw it that it had been meant for them. "You are very good to make the offer," Robert Graham was saying. "Of course we would expect to pay some rent too, even though our title is caretakers. The children loved the place at once. Do I understand that its official name is the Red House? It looks to me like a very good place to settle down to write a book."

Kent's face grew brighter and brighter. "At one time I thought that the place up there was especially good for working because there were no neighbors. Now I find I could very well do with some. And my brother Andrew is coming to visit me a little later. He is, I think, about a year older than Nina. He'll want to know you. Clyde's grandmother, Mrs. Gregory, will come down to help you with cleaning, and I'll go to the village now and send someone up to turn on the water and the electricity. Mrs. Gregory is a good soul; she takes care of my apartment up there and does some cooking. But I don't allow her in my laboratory, she has such a passion for putting things in order that I can never find them. Can we call this all settled then. You won't think that you have to go farther?"

"Yes, it's all settled," Robert Graham told him. "The fact is that we can't go farther, we have to stay here for a time at least. I think I'd better tell you why. You say you know something about me, then perhaps you will not jump to the conclusion that we are thieves."

"Thieves?" echoed Kent. He had got up to go, but he turned back and sat down. "I think I ought to understand about this," he said.

For answer Professor Graham motioned to Nina and Jeff to bring in the leather boxes from the kitchen. He opened them and shook their contents out on the table. "We found these—" he began.

But Kent Clark jumped up and in two long strides was at the door. "Don't tell me about them! I don't want to hear about them!" he cried out. "No, I never saw them before, I wish I'd never seen them. I wish you had never seen them." In a moment more he was outside and had shut the door behind him.

They all sat staring after him and then at one another. "The one thing he didn't say," Jane Graham said, "was that he wished he had never seen us, though I believe that was what he was thinking."

Why the sight of the jewels should have upset Kent so was very hard to guess. "Do you think now he wants us to go away?" Nina asked anxiously. "But he said he wanted us for neighbors."

Inside of an hour, however, a man arrived who said he was to attend to the water and the electricity and put their house in proper shape for their living there. "Kent Clark sent me," he said. "Glad to see someone living in one of the Clark houses again. Reckon you're going to stay with us awhile?" Robert Graham said he reckoned they would.

The next morning Mrs. Gregory arrived, with Casey trotting behind her. Evidently there had been forgiveness on both sides and the affair of the bacon had been forgotten. Arthur rushed out and the two dogs had what Mrs. Graham called a bark-about, running after each other in circles and yelping as they ran.

"Kent told me to make sure that you had everything the way you wanted," Mrs. Gregory announced. She was small and neat and quick, pretty for an old lady and with crinkly white hair. "He didn't say just what to do," she went on. "I knew you'd want to use the big library room, and he didn't know that it needed—well, a sort of a clearing out."

Nina's eyes gleamed as she and her brother followed Mrs. Gregory, who unlocked the door of the room at the back of the house. "Surely she'll tell us all about what it means," Nina thought. But when she offered one question after another, the little old lady only shook her head. "I don't know any better than you what their Uncle Charley had in mind when he set this table out, for he did it all himself, and in the night. Then he came up himself and asked me about a cake. Fortunately I had baked one, a fruit cake—that was his favorite. I knew his birthday was coming. I was all struck of a heap when I came in to clean the next day and found he was gone and saw that everything was still here. I locked up the room and saved everything in its place, thinking for sure that he would be right back. But he never came and neither did any of the others."

Mr. Charley had evidently lived in the Red House, but she would not talk about him nor of those that she spoke of as "the others." She seemed to feel that it was not proper to give information about her employers. "Worked for the family ever since I was out of grade school," she did tell them. "Loved them every one, and Kent too, though he was a cousin and didn't live here. I go up now almost every day to where he's working and put his rooms in order and leave him something cooked, but he won't let me touch a thing in his work place. Laws a mercy, what a sight of disorder it is! I think he spends half his time looking for things that've got out of sight, pushed behind other things. His brother Andy is coming to stay with him while their parents are in the Southwest. I don't know just what the boy will do with himself with Kent working all day and most of the night."

"He must come down to play with us," Jeff said, and Mrs. Gregory nodded, "Yes, he'd like that."

She made short work of the unhappy birthday feast, carefully putting into the kitchen cupboard everything that could be used again. The big birthday cake she put into a basket to carry home for, being a fruit cake, it would keep. Nina and Jeff helped her move the heavy table back near the wall and turn the room into a library again. Daddy will like to sit down and write, Nina thought. Mrs. Gregory, having given the whole house a good cleaning and leaving it exquisitely neat, went trotting away with the basket on her arm and the whole family went joyfully to work at unpacking.

The morning after this, Nina and her father were taking an early walk up the winding, grass-grown driveway with its big trees on each side. They came round a turn quickly and were face to face with Kent, evidently out to take the morning air, too, before he set to work. He stopped short when he came in sight of them, muttered something that might be called a good morning, turned abruptly and plunged into the woods beside the road. Nina looked after him in wonder. "He doesn't want to speak to us," she declared in wonder. "And only two days ago he wanted us foi neighbors!"

Professors learn, through their teaching, a great deal about the minds and hearts of young people and how to understand them. Robert Graham was particularly wise at looking into young men's thoughts, since he had come so close to so many of them. He stood, deeply distressed, looking after Kent. "Those jewels have been a great trouble to us, even in the short time since we found them," he said. "But whatever they have to do with that boy —and we cannot guess what it is—they are coming near to breaking his heart. And I don't see how we can do anything to help him."

But Nina could not believe that they were so helpless. "We have to do something," she answered. "Surely we can do something. Even children can sometimes do something." And a thought deep inside her said also, I would like to help him. And I would like to get to know Toots.

"If we want to help put things right," her father was saying, "we would have to know first what is wrong. To find that out would be hard to do. But it's true that children can be very good at finding out things."

5

The Island Rock

"I think," said Robert Graham as he and Nina stood at the door of the Red House on the next morning, before breakfast, "that I can certainly recommend New England summer weather. We've made a very good choice of a climate to spend the next months in." Three days did not make a very complete record to judge from, but it could not be denied that so far the weather had been all that anybody could ask. He and Nina were about to take an early walk, "And we won't disturb Kent's before-breakfast stroll," Robert Graham said, "We'll just go out through the driveway and down the road this time."

The air was so clear that it sparkled and Nina skipped along beside her father, full of that pleasant feeling that everything in the world would turn out well on such a day as this. They were on their way back when they stopped a minute to look at the glorious view spread out before them, the great curve of the valley, the fold upon fold of mountains marching away into the distance. As they stood there a man came down the road from its steeper stretch above, a round stout man, with red hair touched with gray that curled tight all over his head. He wore such a battered hat that Nina thought he might have borrowed it from the scarecrow in the field.

"Mornin'," he said cheerily as he went by, then turned round to speak further. "You're mebbe Professor Graham that's come to live at the Red House. Kent Clark just told me I was to come and cut your grass and clean up the weeds and all like that. I'll be coming round to do it one of these days now."

"I think you'd better be about it, then," Robert Graham said, rather severely. He evidently knew a lazy man when he saw one. "The grass looks like destruction and it's getting worse every day. How about coming in to do it now?"

"Why," the man seemed surprised and pained at such haste. "I expect I could do it today, if you're in that much of a rush. I have an errand in the town this morning, but I'll come sure this afternoon. I've worked for the Clarks a long time, not quite so long as Amanda Gregory, but it's getting to be a good while. I've got a house up the hill from hers, the gardener's house they call it, though I work inside the big house and out, when they are here. My name is Barney Gates." Nina and her father had walked on toward home and he had walked beside them, until they came to the Red House driveway. As they turned in, Barney Gates was saying, "The mower's in the shed, I take it, like always—" He would have stood there talking longer, but Robert Graham said finally, "We'll see you this afternoon then. Good morning," and went in.

"Kent does think about us," Nina said, as they came up on the porch, and her father answered, "He does indeed. He sent the plumber and the telephone man and above all, he sent Mrs. Gregory. Your mother says she's almost as great a piece of good fortune as the Red House itself."

They were to have further proof of Kent's thoughtfulness that same morning when Nina went with her father to do some errands in the village. They were stopped, as they walked across the village green, by the young man whom they recognized as the bank president who, on that first day, had turned them away. He said now: "Young Kent Clark came in yesterday and said that he knew all about you and that the bank could not have a better customer. I regret very much that there was a little misunderstanding at the beginning. We would be glad indeed to serve you now in any way possible."

For a moment Nina thought that her father would refuse the services of the bank, but the stiff look on his face relaxed and he smiled warmly. "I find, after all, that I am stopping here for some time," he answered graciously. "So I'll bring down my valuables and put them in one of your safety boxes, immediately." They all walked together across the green toward the bank. On the way, they passed a bench where Barney Gates was sitting, puffing at a short pipe and sitting with a rather shabby-looking friend, both laughing uproariously at each other's jokes. The bank president, whose name they had learned was George Sylvester, greeted him warmly as they went by. "I expect you've got acquainted with Barney by now," he said to Robert Graham. "He's worked up at the place on Clark's Hill so long that he's got to be just about a part of it. He's the laziest man that ever lived, and everyone likes him. He's a wonderful gardener, there isn't anything he doesn't know about flowers and fruit, and about wind and weather. I've heard he's a good house man, too, in his own way, which is never to do a job until he absolutely has to and then to do it extraordinarily well."

"Yes," Robert Graham said without any enthusiasm. He evidently was going to wait until all this was proved. They went into the bank. Nina's father went in to sign some papers, then hurried her out and into the car. They drove up the hill at top speed, and he rushed in to open the door of the smallest kitchen cupboard which, happily, had a lock on it. He had made up a brown paper parcel holding all the leather boxes and he gave this to Nina to hold as they went dashing down the hill again and drew up before the bank. George Sylvester looked a little startled at such a rapid way of doing business, but he took them into the big vault, set them up with a safety deposit box and stood by while the package was put in it and the box closed with a satisfying click.

When they got home Robert Graham stood for a moment on the front step, stretched his arms wide and said happily, "I'm a free man again, and don't have the weight of a fortune in jewels hanging on me at every turn. In the end we'll have to find out to whom they belong, but for a time at least I'm going to take a vacation from jewels. I intend to have a little time and thought to spend on myself and my book. Am I right in understanding that the family has voted that the library is to be mine, for writing? If somebody will bring me in some sandwiches for lunch, I'll just disappear now, and not see the rest of you until dinnertime. My first section has to be finished by the end of the month and it is going round and round in my head." He went into his room, unpacked his typewriter, and about ten minutes later they could hear him clicking away at great speed to make up for lost time.

Jane Graham went out into the kitchen, followed by Nina. Her mother was smiling happily to herself. They had set out on their journey to look for a good place for writing a book and now they had found it.

"I'm going to bake a cake," she said to Nina, "and I don't have quite enough eggs. Could you go up and ask Mrs. Gregory for some, there's just time to do it before lunch." Nina was quite willing. She always wanted more chance to talk to Mrs. Gregory. If she were careful and asked the right questions she might learn more about Toots. Since she did not yet have anyone else to play with she had more or less taken Toots for her best friend. Toots was one of the three for whom the treasure hunt had been planned, but that was all that she knew so far. She was determined to know more, and perhaps knowing more might lead to solving the puzzle about the jewels and why Kent was so upset at the sight of them. Jeff decided that he would like to go with her; "Arthur wanted to play awhile with Casey," he said.

They trudged up the hill and very soon came to the cottage where Clyde and his grandmother lived. It looked just right, small, with a steep roof and bright flowers on each side of the door. Nina knocked and Mrs. Gregory came quickly to let her in. "I was just thinking about all of you," she said. "I'm churning butter and I wanted to send some down to your mother, nice and fresh made. It'll be done in about five minutes. I just have to work the buttermilk out of it." Nina sat down beside the low window to wait. Outside, Jeff was looking for Clyde and Casey.

"Do you like being at the Red House?" Mrs. Gregory asked. Nina had expected just that question and had made up her answer as she came up the road. "We do like it. There are such wonderful places to play, by the brook and in the orchard. Jeff and I love it and the—the others must have loved it too. Was—was Toots the youngest?"

"Yes," Mrs. Gregory was answering without thinking. "They were all so happy here. Toots is the youngest, about your age or maybe a few months older. She is yellow-haired and blue-eyed, not with dark hair and gray eyes like you."

Nina sat as still as a mouse. She was actually going to hear more about Toots, but suddenly, Jeff, outside the window asked, "Where's Clyde, where's Casey?"

"Oh Jeff, you shouldn't interrupt like that," Nina cried out, for she felt that the chance of hearing something that she so much wanted to know was quite lost now. She spoke more sharply than she intended and Jeff did not answer so very politely because his feelings were hurt.

"I didn't hear you saying anything so very wonderful yourself," he returned hotly.

"Oh don't, *don't* quarrel!" Mrs. Gregory cried

out. They were not really quarreling; Nina had been sorry the moment that she spoke. But they seemed to have upset Mrs. Gregory very badly. "I always told the boys," she said, "that's George and Charley—they're men now but it was when they were boys they used to snap at each other and go to quarreling. I used to say to them, 'You think it's all right now, and soon over, but when you are men it won't be so easy to make an end.' They laughed at me, but see what happened when they—" She broke off, she was very near to crying, Nina thought, and tried to comfort her.

"Don't mind, Mrs. Gregory. Jeff and I didn't mean anything."

"Sure we didn't," Jeff said and raced off, for he saw Clyde and Casey coming across the yard.

"You mustn't mind me, my dear," the old lady said, but her voice was still trembling. "Now the butter is ready and I'll just put up the eggs your mother wanted." There was no hope of getting her back to talk of Toots, Nina was sure, so she held the bowl while Mrs. Gregory pressed the butter into a neat round pat. "Just like what Red Riding Hood took to her grandmother," the little old lady said, as she put it into a bag. Nina thanked her, bade her good-by, called Jeff, and went thoughtfully home.

It was the next day that Nina and Jeff had set aside to do more exploring than there had been time for before. Their mother had lunch early for them so that they should have a long afternoon. When they came out into the garden, the pleasant sound of a lawn mower was going back and forth, for Barney Gates, who had not come yesterday as he had promised, was at last at work on the grass. Jeff had come out first, and the mower stopped while Barney very willingly paused to talk to him. He and Barney were both laughing when Nina came up. "That's a nice funny man," Jeff said as they walked away together. "But he says he hates to cut grass. He says time is slower than a wet week when he hasn't anybody to talk to."

They were just going out of the gate when Barney called after them. "Don't go too far, it's going to rain. There was a ring around the moon last night."

Nothing seemed more unlikely than that it might rain. It was still, clear weather, with the mountains standing brilliant blue across the valley looking "so near you could almost touch them," Jeff said. He and Arthur seemed to have no special plan except to run here and there and follow any path and see where it might lead. Nina, however, had a more definite purpose in mind. She wanted to find a quiet and empty place where she could sit down and have a good space of time to think about all the puzzling and disturbing things that seemed to be going on around her. It seemed to her that a good place for thinking would be the "Island Rock with its crown of ferns," to which they had been led by the treasure hunt clue. But when they came to the brook Jeff wanted to go downstream to the meadow and the orchard, so Nina turned the other way and began trudging uphill. The water of the brook beside her was deep and swift, as such mountain brooks are and was full of sound and a music all its own.

Once she stopped and listened, for she thought that she heard someone else going through the woods farther up the hill. Yes, it did seem as though she heard footsteps at some distance away; she even thought that she heard somebody whistling. But although she stood still to listen, the sound, whatever it was, went away in another direction and she heard no more. It could not have been Jeff. He and Arthur had very definitely gone downhill—Arthur was in hot pursuit of a squirrel which ran along overhead from tree to tree, chattering and scolding and teasing the dog, who yelped and leaped but could not hope to reach him.

And now the stream made a sharp turn and she had come to the Island Rock, standing stark and gray in the middle of the rushing water. As she remembered, the sides were high and slippery and she had some trouble in getting over the stepping stones. The water was deeper, she noted, than when she had been there before, and it was not easy to get over dry-shod. The great trees crowded so thickly here, and hung so far down over the water that she could hardly see the sky overhead where a big black cloud was spreading and giving promise of rain. She was too much occupied in making progress, for the water foamed and splashed about her as she picked her way across to the foot of the rock and below the stream plunged suddenly downward into a deep quiet pool. Without Jeff's help she found it was not easy to get up the side of the rock, which was as high as her head, but at last she had scrambled up, and sat down at the foot of a little thorn tree which had somehow twisted its roots into cracks in the stone and so had been able to grow to some size. Everywhere else were little bushes and moss and the green nodding ferns.

She sat down on a cushion of moss and leaned her head back against the trunk of the small tree. She could think now, fully and quietly, and her mind went back to the puzzle of the jewels. Who had put them into the well? Why had that person never come back to get them? It would be wonderful if she and Jeff could find it all out, to tell the others, to get the brilliant stones of red and green and blue back to their rightful owner. What could they do to help and comfort Kent, working away in his laboratory, too busy to keep things in order, pushing on day after day to finish the experiment that he had promised Professor Craig to complete? Little by little her ideas got away from her and ran from one impossible scheme to another. The whole affair was fantastic, not only their finding the jewels, but the fact that Kent, who had been so grateful and friendly when they first met him, had suddenly come to avoid them. Even Mrs. Gregory would not help them by telling what she knew—all were puzzles of these last few days. Her thoughts wandered farther and farther away.

A sudden little spatter of rain aroused her to what was going on about her, and the spatter was followed by a great crack of thunder overhead, and then by a blinding downpour, beating down all around, flattening the ferns, soaking her clothes, turning her hair into wet strings that hung into her eyes. The great black cloud had seemed to drop its whole contents directly upon her and with no warning except for the single crack of thunder.

One portion of the rock was higher than the rest and overhung a little, so that she could crawl into a sort of shelter, but the little tree pitched and groaned as the wind snatched at it, and the roar of the stream grew louder and louder. She made herself as small as she could, drawing up her feet under her and putting her head down on her arms, feeling herself grow colder and wetter every minute. It was one of those sudden mountain-side storms of which she had never before had experience, it seemed as though the whole of the sky overhead had dissolved to come down upon her.

But, like all such mountain storms, it lasted not more than a few minutes, then the lash of the rain began to move away across the woods; the curtain of falling drops all about her grew thinner and thinner; the clouds began to break overhead. But when she moved at last and peered over the edge of the rock she saw that the water had risen, that the brook was a foaming torrent now, pouring down in wild and furious force. "How will I get back?" she wondered wildly.

Very carefully she let herself down over the side of the rock, holding to one of the hard small roots of the thorn tree, and put one foot on the first stepping stone. Immediately it was swept out from under her so that it was only her grip on the tree root that kept her from being swept down to the deep pool below. She tried again, but this time came so close to being sucked into the roaring water that it was only with the very last bit of her strength that she pulled herself back by the friendly root and, by desperate struggle, managed to get back to the top of the rock again. Looking over the side she could see that the water was coming up steadily as measured on the great stone. She noticed something she had not seen before, that the banks of the stream were so steep and high that the water could easily rise to the point of flowing over the rock on which she stood.

"Jeff," she called, "Jeff." But she felt sure that he could never hear her voice above the tumult of the water.

"And if he does come," she began to think, "what could he do? He could never get over to

help me, he would only be washed away. But he could go and get somebody who is bigger."

She waited, quiet now, too desperate and too hoarse to cry out again. She was terrified when she heard a crashing in the bushes. She had meant to tell Jeff that he must go to fetch someone to help her, but would she be able to make him understand? Suddenly she saw Arthur, dripping wet, come out at the water's edge, then saw her brother break his way through the underbrush to follow his dog. He shouted to her and she tried to answer, to tell him what to do. But neither one could hear the other, and she saw him wade in, knee-deep.

"Go back!" she cried with all the breath that was left in her, "Go back, go back!"

6

The Laboratory

Jeff and Arthur had been having a wonderful morning in the woods. A boy and a young dog can have a dozen good ideas about what directions to follow up and down the green rustling pathways. Once or twice Jeff's conscience pricked him a little, for he really knew that his mother, when she told him that he might go, had meant that he and Nina should keep together. These woods were still strange and they had not yet explored them fully. He was sure, however, that Nina could take good care of herself, although the truth was that she was less able to do so than her sharp-eyed, alert, younger brother. He was not given to daydreaming in unfamiliar places.

And he very soon forgot about his sister in the great interest of making a new acquaintance. He and Arthur were just beginning to get a little tired of aimless running to and fro, when he came across a boy, a good deal taller than himself, and perhaps some years older, sitting on a flat rock, fishing in the brook. Jeff stopped short. "Hullo," he said. "You're Andrew aren't you? Catching anything?"

The other boy answered in his turn, "Hullo. Yes, I'm Andrew. My brother Kent has been telling me about you, so I expect you're Jeff. No, I'm not catching anything, the water's not right and the fish aren't biting."

Jeff came over to him without hesitation and sat down beside him. "Where's Nina?" Andrew asked. "Do you like it at the Red House?"

"We love it," Jeff answered, answering the last question first and with much enthusiasm. "And Nina—I don't exactly know where she is right now. Somewhere up there in the woods."

They sat there on the stone together for a while, asking and answering the questions that lead to further acquaintance. Jeff said, finally, "Why hasn't Kent brought you down to see us?"

"I only just came," Andrew answered, "and I told him twice today that I wanted to go down to your house, but he said he was too busy and couldn't I go alone. I didn't just want to walk in on strangers and say 'Look, I'm Andy Clark,' so I stopped to fish awhile and make up my mind."

"Well, do come now," Jeff urged, but Andrew looked up at the sky and said, "It's going to rain, and rain hard. We'd best, both of us, be getting home." Jeff looked at the sky also, but with a less practiced eye than Andy's.

"Oh, not for quite a while, anyway," he insisted, but Andrew was reeling in his line and getting up.

"Kent's working so hard he won't think to shut the windows," he said. "So I'll see you."

He walked away up the path and Jeff and Arthur went running off in the opposite direction down toward the orchard.

When the rain began, as Andrew had said it would, Jeff stood still, not able to make up his mind. Ought he to go and find Nina, and see that she started home before she got too wet? Then, when the skies seemed to open and the rain came down in blinding sheets, he turned and ran, not toward home but up the hill, calling "Nina, Nina." He must find her, he had to find her. Anything might happen to her in such a rain. Arthur, a very damp and subdued dog, plodded along at his heels.

The farther he ran, through bushes that were thick, tangled and thorny, the more determined he became to get to her, no matter where she was. She had spoken of the Island Rock, and wanting to see it again. He pushed, very wearily now, in the direction where he thought it was.

When at last Nina saw Jeff come out on the shore, her anxiety for herself turned into terror for him. She tried by wild gestures to get him to go back. But he had only one idea, to get across to her. She looked away, she could not watch, and then suddenly a loud sharp barking on the bank made her turn around again.

The dog Casey was there among the rocks, jumping up and down and yelping wildly. Then a boy came out behind him, a boy she had never seen before. "Hi," he called.

"Hi," Nina answered. It was a very faint and hoarse little call. She knew the boy must be Andrew Clark because he looked like his brother and was the right size. He came down to stand on the rock opposite her, reached out and caught Jeff's arm where he stood knee-deep in the rushing water, and drew him back. Jeff protested and struggled but to her great relief, the bigger boy got him back on shore. Yet her relief was short, for in a minute Andrew had plunged in to try to come across.

Immediately the force of the white water whirled him off his feet and he reeled and staggered. If he had not been quick enough to catch at the branch of a tree that dipped into the water, he would have been carried away, down to the deep pool. He pulled himself out with difficulty and got back to the bank. Not even the dog Casey had dared to follow him into the water. Arthur stood on a big stone, whimpering, with one foot raised.

Andrew seemed to convince Jeff that there was no use in plunging in again and he stopped struggling. The bigger boy shouted something that Nina at last could hear, "I'll get somebody," and turned away dashing into the bushes with Casey behind him.

Jeff sat down disconsolately, with the rain streaming off him and with Arthur pressed close to his side. Nina tried to find a slightly drier spot under the shelter of the little thorn tree. It was quite true that Jeff could do nothing but watch her helplessly, yet it was a comfort, just the same, to have someone near.

They did not have very long to wait, before they heard feet crashing through the bushes again. Andrew came into sight first with someone behind him. Nina had hoped that it might be her father, but it was not. It was Kent Clark. She realized that his place was nearer and he would be the first person Andrew would turn to. Even in her wet misery she smiled a little to herself. I did not have a chance to send him a message on an egg, she was thinking.

Kent Clark stood for a moment on the bank, not hesitating, but looking for the surest place to set his first step. He had picked up a heavy stick and now used it to feel the way, to find which stones were firm and which were rocking in the great rush of water. He came forward bravely, yet staggering more than once as he slipped and nearly fell. He reached the biggest of the flat stones at the foot of the rock and stood on it holding to the root of the thorn tree.

"Go carefully," he directed as Nina came out from her small shelter and moved toward him. Even though he was so near, he had to raise his voice to be heard. "Come here to the edge. I'll catch you if you slip. Now, slide down," he said, when she stood above him. "Don't be afraid. I'm here to see you don't fall. I will turn round and take you on my back."

He lurched a little as her weight came down on his shoulders, but he did not lose his balance. "Don't move if you can help it, and keep your eyes shut."

She could feel that he was leaning to one side, to stand fast against the force of the roaring water. It seemed as though they went a long way before he stood still, and she opened her eyes to see Andrew and Jeff on each side, leaning down to help as they came up the bank. Kent set her down and she stood shivering and trembling, really more frightened now than she had been at any time before.

"It's all right," Kent was saying. He turned to Jeff, "I'm going to take her up to my place, it's the nearest. Mrs. Gregory is there and will see that she gets dry. You go down to your house and tell your father and mother that she's safe and will come home a little later."

"I'll come with you," Andrew said. Those short

moments beside the brook had seemed to make them fast friends. They ran off together.

When Nina came up the stairs, Mrs. Gregory made a great fuss over her and drew her into the little apartment beyond the laboratory. Nina was not too upset to note, as she walked through, the wild disorder of Kent's work place, with bottles stacked together any which way. Notes and papers were scattered about, instruments were lying here and there, some of which she knew by name, some not. She had enjoyed going with her father to his chemist friend's laboratory; she had even learned to help a little in washing test tubes and cleaning things, while the two professors sat and talked.

Mrs. Gregory whisked her into the kitchen and set her down before the open door of the oven. "You warm yourself a little here, before we do anything else," she said. She gave Nina a cup of hot soup to drink and then, somehow, she disappeared, though for not more than twenty minutes. She came in again, in her raincoat, dripping, and carrying a bundle under her arm. Nina heard Kent say, outside in the laboratory, "Why, Mrs. Gregory, did you go over to the big house? Did you find what Nina needed?"

"Everything is just hanging in the closets," Mrs. Gregory answered. "It's just as though they had all stepped out for an hour and would be right back again, instead of its being months they have been gone. I just took the key off the nail there and went in the back way. Didn't you say Barney Gates was to go in and keep the place clean? He hasn't been near it, I'll be bound. Everything is deep in dust."

She helped Nina put on the dry clothes and zipped up the neat red dress that was only a little too large. Nina waited until her shoes were a little drier, then said to Mrs. Gregory, "Thank you so much for the soup and the clothes. I think I had better go home now. Will I—will I disturb Kent if I go out through the laboratory?"

"Not if you go quietly and don't stop to talk," Mrs. Gregory said a little anxiously. "He works so hard and every day he gets more touchy about being disturbed. Working himself to death, he is, and not for any reason that I can see. There's just something on his mind, I believe, that he's trying to get away from."

Nina tiptoed out, meaning to be as silent as a mouse, but Kent heard her and turned around from what he was doing. She had not really seen before how tired he looked and how unhappy. He was shaking something shiny up and down in a bottle. She forgot that she was not supposed to speak and exclaimed, "Oh, you're cleaning mercury. I know how to do that, Dr. Baron used to let me help him. Could I—could I help you now?"

He looked at her doubtfully. "Are you sure you know how? You won't spill the acid you use for cleaning it? I have this whole jug to clean and I want to get on to something else."

"I do know how and I'd love to do it," she answered joyfully and without more ado she climbed up on the high stool and set to work. She had always loved the quicksilver brightness, and the heavy feel of the smooth mercury, and the way it separated into round fat drops. Mrs. Gregory peeped in and then went away with a look of wonder on her kind old face. It was fully an hour before Kent spoke to Nina again.

"You've certainly done enough for now, and you must be very tired," he said. "They'll want to hear at home about your adventure in the brook. But if you would really like—you could help me again."

"I'll come back for my clothes," she called to Mrs. Gregory as she ran across the room to the stairs. At the top of them she turned back. "I never thanked you—" she began, but Kent had already turned back to his test tube not seeming to hear her. As she went down the stairs Nina happened to put her hand into the pocket of the dress and pulled out a neatly and squarely folded handkerchief. It was marked in the corner "Toots." She nodded to herself. She was not surprised.

It seemed the most natural thing in the world that Nina was presently going up to Kent's laboratory every day that Mrs. Gregory did. She would set to work without many words at what so greatly needed to be done. Kent would look up and nod a morning or an afternoon greeting and perhaps say, "Over there are the bottles and basins I need the most. They do sort of need cleaning, but don't try to put them in order." She obeyed his directions carefully, so that the place was still in much the same kind of confusion that Kent seemed to like. But at least things were clean and at hand when he needed them. There was one afternoon when he seemed not quite so busy as before and he looked up and said, "When you get to be bigger and go to college, you're going to be a very good girl in a laboratory. Are you going to be a chemist too? To my mind it's the best science of all."

She shook her head. "I like a laboratory better where things are alive."

He was looking at her with the old friendliness of that first day before he caught sight of the jewels and everything had changed so suddenly. He was smiling now, as he stood up reaching for a small bottle that stood on a special shelf above the counter. Nina knew that all those in that row were something very particular and she had been most careful never to touch them. "This is a rather special day for me," Kent said as he went back to his working place and unscrewed the top of the bottle. He began weighing out some of the powder from it in his small, delicate scales. They were so true in their measuring, he had once shown her, that you could weigh a slip of paper, then write your name on it, and it would be heavier in the scale pan than when you had weighed it before. She was sure he would not want to talk to her further so she picked up a tray full of jars and tubes and went away to the kitchen. It was a dark day outside, the beginning of late afternoon. She must try to finish quickly for it would soon be time for her and Mrs. Gregory to go home.

She was just coming back, with her task finished and carrying the tray when she heard a sudden exclamation from Kent. "Oh, no," he cried out. "Not that one, not that one too!" She set her load down carefully, and ran over to his side.

"What is it?" she asked anxiously. "What's wrong?"

He had lighted a burner under a test tube full of the powder, and it was bubbling away, giving out an odd sound and smell. The room had grown very shadowy and she saw, as his face bent over the small light, how all his cheerfulness and his smile were gone. For a minute he did not answer, and then his words came tumbling out as though he had to tell someone.

"It may be that my whole work of the summer will come to nothing," he said. "It may all end in nothing. Yes, I'll have done what Professor Craig wanted me to do, but it won't really have helped him." He drew a long breath. Nina was afraid he would not say any more, but go back to his work in silence. But no, he was going to explain. "Professor Craig gave me a whole list of chemicals to test, to see if they would be of use to him in a big project in medicine that he's carrying out. I've been working them over, one after another, and each one has proved to be of no use at all. I've tried more than half of them, and haven't found one that was what we were looking for. I had hoped the most for this one, but the first test doesn't look like much. I sometimes wonder if it's any use going on at all."

"But you wanted to get your scholarship, you wanted to go back to Highgate to study," Nina said. She knew that he did. She herself wanted him to be able to, had wanted it ever since that first day they began to know him.

"Oh, I want to go on studying," he answered drearily. "But more than anything else I want to help Dr. Craig. He has been so good to me and this thing he is doing is so very big. It seems that I must, I absolutely must, find something of the kind that he needs. I can't think about anything else until I do. I—I know you are all worried about the jewels and things, but I just can't think about anything until this is settled."

He seemed to have talked himself into a better mood, for he took up his work again. The room had got quite dark now and he lighted the bulb directly over his head. And then to Nina's surprise he asked her to help him.

"If you just stand here to hold this glass beaker and let the liquid go into the test tube, drop by drop, that would keep my hands free for the rest of the test. I know you have a steady hand, you haven't dropped or broken anything since you began to work here. Now, just one drop at a time." He put the little pitcher-shaped glass into her hand. "Hold it so and let it drip—drip—" He bent to his work again hardly knowing that she was there.

Nina caught a glimpse of Mrs. Gregory coming to the door, looking in, and then going quietly back into the kitchen. It was just possible to see her, sitting now, waiting, with her hands in her lap, perfectly willing to stay as long as Kent might need Nina's help. Kent looked up at last and drew a long breath.

"I believe I was wrong," he said. "This might be the one." His voice was shaking with excite-

ment. "Oh, if it could be, if it only could be! I'll have to go on and test out the rest, because I promised Dr. Craig that I would. And then I can come back to this. I do believe that this may be what he wants. Thank you, it was a real help. And now I must let you and Mrs. Gregory go home."

Next morning when she came in with Mrs. Gregory, Kent hardly looked up, he was so hard at work. Had he forgotten all about the afternoon before, Nina wondered. It seemed to her that he looked discouraged again, but she knew enough not to ask any questions. And presently, when he seemed to have come to a stopping place, he straightened up on his stool and looked at her.

"You mustn't think that I don't take notice of all you do for me," he said. "You told me a while ago that you liked a laboratory where things were alive, didn't you? I could make room for a jar of tadpoles or some such things, and you could watch them grow into frogs. You might enjoy having something of your own."

"Oh, I would," she returned eagerly. "I'll go down to the brook right now and look for some." She poked her head into the kitchen door and said to Mrs. Gregory, "I'm going to look for tadpoles. I won't be long."

Although she and Jeff had spent some time in the woods, they had not explored them everywhere. They had found a fishing spot for the boys, a wading place for her, and even a long pool of very cold water for swimming. But she had never followed the whole course of the stream directly, and she set out to do so now, so that she might look in any quiet stretch for darting tadpoles. She went upstream first, farther than she had ever been before, until a dark wall of rock, with the stream dropping over one edge of it, stood up in her way. There were thick brambles all along the barrier of rock, with vines and bushes hanging down from above. I expect there are no tadpoles up there, she decided and turned to go downstream again. She passed the place where she had begun to follow the brook and came down, she thought, fairly near to where the stream made its sudden turn above the Island Rock. Then she stopped suddenly. She had never seen this.

7

The Water Garden

Nina stood, looking at this stretch of quiet water, in a reach of the brook she had not come across before. The shore was fairly level, not like the rocky banks farther downstream and below the Island Rock. The stream ran singing among the the big stones with their smooth covering of brown water, for the roots of trees and bushes and ferns had given it a color of its very own. Beside the brook, reaching inward on the lower ground, was a wide, shallow pool, about the length and width of a good-sized room. All about it was a frame of plants and flowers. Big cattails made a tall border, below them were arrowheads with pointed leaves and small creamy blossoms, and below them in turn were sheets of blue forget-me-nots, clumps of blue and yellow iris and other flowers whose names Nina did not know. In the middle of the pool, rocking on the ripples, were scattered the wide-open many-petaled pond lilies, white ones, pale pink, and deep rose. How could they all be blooming here together, just by accident, she was wondering. Then she began to notice that the whole pool, with its wreath of flowers, was exactly round, something that could not be by chance.

"I wonder if there are fish in it," she thought and knelt down at the edge to look. Yes, there were fish, dashing here and there, some larger, some smaller, but nothing that looked all head and slim tail which would be tadpoles. There were, instead, a great many tiny fishes with stumpy tails, circling in and out of the floating leaves and grass at such speed that she could hardly catch proper sight of them. And then it suddenly occurred to her that she had come in such a hurry she hadn't brought anything to carry them home in.

A big willow tree stood just where the pool bordered the running brook, and as she came round the stout trunk she drew back suddenly for someone was there. She saw a broad stooping back, a red head and battered hat—it was Barney Gates. He stood up quickly for such a stout man, and smiled broadly at her.

"You found it, did you?" he said. "I wondered

when you would, for you were bound to. I was going to get it all cleared out of weeds before you came across it, so it would be the way Toots kept it."

Toots's garden! She might have known. In that minute she seemed to know more about Toots than in all the days before when she had been trying to find out about her. "Did she plant it herself?" she asked Barney.

"I helped her," he said. "There's a wall of stones there you see, that cuts it off from the brook but lets the water through. She couldn't have done it very easily herself, though I'm bound she would have managed it in the end. And some of the plants she didn't know where to look for, and I showed her. That white moccasin flower, that's very rare, but I happened to stumble over the place where they grow. And that yellow wood lily, you don't come across that very often now." He showed her the two plants, the fairy white, slipper-shaped flower, and the delicate yellow lily blossom. "She got most of it planted before I found her working on it," Barney ended, "but the brook would come in and tear things out."

After that he shut his lips firmly, just like Mrs. Gregory, and would say no more. She asked him questions but he only shook his head. She began to speak of other things and then moved the talk back to the garden and Toots, but he neatly turned the conversation away again, and she could not stop him. She told him what she had come for and he said, "There's not any tadpoles here that I've seen." She would like to take some of the stumpy-tailed fishes then, she said but remembered again that she had nothing to carry them in. "They're so tiny, my shoe will do," she announced and sat down to take off her rubber-soled sneaker, dipping out a whole group of the little darting fishes. "I'll have to go back quickly before the water leaks out," she said to Barney, but she stopped for one last attempt. "You might tell me about her," she said. "You know how much I want her for my friend—even though I can't see her. You might tell me just a little of what I want to know."

He only turned away, bending his broad back again to the forget-me-nots. He spoke at last, stooping down over them. His voice was not only sad, but it was pitiful. "They're such a fine family, every one of them, and we don't know if they'll ever come back. I miss them so—Toots the most. I—I can't speak about them." Nina could not ask any more questions. She could only go.

She ran most of the way back, but very unevenly with one foot bare. She got to the laboratory breathless, but with the fish still swimming. Kent actually put down what he was doing to come and look. "Guppies!" he said. "Toots used to have guppies." He caught himself suddenly; it was not what he meant to say. He would not go on, but he helped Nina find the biggest glass jar that was empty and even held the shoe while she ran to wash the jar out and fill it with water. Together they set it safely on a broad shelf. She stood watching the fish so long that she was suddenly ashamed, remembering that she was only invited there to help wash things for Kent. She hurriedly put on the big blue apron Mrs. Gregory had made for her and set busily to work. She had to go and look at the guppies every now and again, to see whether they were settling down in their new home. They seemed to be fully satisfied and swept round and round in their endless circles quite content with where they had now come to live.

"There ought to be some water weeds down in the pond that you could put in with them," Kent said. "They need something green to keep the water pure."

"I'll get some before I come up again," she said. She found it hard to leave when Mrs. Gregory said it was time to go home.

The next day was Sunday and they all went down to the little church whose white spire was the first thing they had seen in Durham village. In the afternoon they took a long drive with more and more of the beauties of the New England hills and valleys unfolding before them. Nina had told her family that first day about the garden by the brook "that somebody had planted." She was a little shy of saying how often she thought about Toots, how she had long imaginary conversations with her as she pictured their playing together. All of her family wanted to see the garden sometime, but her father and mother were too busy to come at once. But Monday Jeff could not wait any longer and insisted that Nina must show it to him. Barney's feet and now hers had worn a real path up through the woods to where it lay. As they came along the brook together Arthur galloped on ahead. Arthur's only use for a garden was as a soft spot where a dog could dig, and when they came up they were horrified to find a large black hole which Arthur was very busy making bigger. Jeff shouted to stop him and the dog sat down proudly, his tongue hanging out. A whole patch of delicate, yellow wood lilies had been torn up and broken to bits. "And Barney said they were hard to get," Nina lamented. "What will we do?"

Barney himself came up the path presently, for he seemed far more willing to put in an afternoon on Toots's garden than on his own or the Grahams'. His face wrinkled with distress when he saw the broken stems and roots of the lily plants. "She set great store by them," he said, pushing his hat forward and scratching the back of his head as he debated what to do.

"Could we possibly find any more?" Nina asked anxiously. She never questioned within her mind that Toots would come back to work in her garden again and to see what was still there and what was missing.

"It seems to me that she told me once where she got them," Barney answered. "It's in my mind that it was way up higher on the hill, above where that big wall of rock is. It would be a good deal of a scramble to get up there, I'm thinking. But well, I'm willing to try it if you are."

It was a hotter day than they had had before. As the three of them went toiling up the steep hill their faces dripped and their hands were wet and slippery when they took hold of bushes and branches to help themselves upward. Nina and Jeff came to the foot of the tall rock face and stood looking up; it seemed impossible to climb it. Barney was a little behind. He came puffing up, crashing through the bushes. "There's a way up here, at one side, beside where the brook goes down," he told them, "but you have to mind your step."

He showed them the way, at the very edge of the plunging water. Nina slipped more than once and got her feet soaking wet; Jeff fell in completely between two boulders and came out dripping. Arthur was the wettest of the three. But nobody minded on such a hot afternoon. Barney was more nimble than anyone would have thought and got out with less mishaps than the others. They were all tired and out of breath when they came finally out on the stretch of level grass at the top, and the backs of their legs were aching. They were glad to sit down to rest a while before looking for flowers.

Arthur, lying beside them, suddenly jumped out, but Barney caught him and put his hand over the dog's mouth to muffle an excited bark. "Don't move, but look over there," he said in a whisper. Opposite them was a large black rock close to the edge of the running water. Something was moving beside it, a small furry animal and then another. Presently a bigger one, dark brown, long and smooth, came up from the stream to join the others. There were four little ones in sight now. "They're mink," Barney whispered, "the mother and her young ones. She's brought them a trout. The wind's the wrong way for her to get our scent."

It seemed now that there were six little ones, although they were hard to count, they moved so fast. Their sharp little underjaws showed white as they rolled over tearing at the fish, and their mother tried to see that they all were fed. It was Arthur who finally broke loose in a frenzy of excitement and rushed upon them, whereupon they all vanished as though by magic under the big rock. After a moment they saw the mother's head pushed a little way out and heard the odd hissing noise by which she was trying to frighten them way. But the instant they stood up, she disappeared.

"They have a good place up here where they're not often disturbed," Barney said. "With such good fishing right at their door, and a dry den under the stone they have pretty comfortable living quarters. They've been breeding here for years, I've seen them many times myself. Well, we'd better get about looking for our flowers."

They found the lilies, lifting their sturdy nodding blossoms in clumps beside the brook. Nina thought she had never seen such a lovely shade in flowers. "Don't dig up more of them than we really need," Barney warned. "We don't want to kill them off."

He took charge of the big clump that they had taken up, and bore them down safely, although Nina and Jeff had all they could do, using both hands, to get down without slipping and rolling over and over. Arthur made the best descent, going down in one wild rush that got him to the bottom right side up in a shower of loose stones. They all stood to watch Barney's skillful hands as he planted the flowers where the old ones had been destroyed, and, with an eye on Arthur, thrust some sharp stakes into the ground around them so that no enterprising dog could do any further digging.

The hot weather held for the next few days, for summer was now well upon them. By evening the cool air from the mountains made all things comfortable again. "And we do have to expect July and August to come around," Robert Graham said. He was in high good spirits, for his book was moving along well and he did not have to complete the first section "until the end of the month." Also his mind was more or less at ease since he knew that the jewels were safe in the bank. "But what we're going to do about them when we leave here to go back to the university, I don't know," he declared. "It looks as though we might have to settle down to watch over the awkward things for the rest of our lives."

Nina and her father stopped, once, to make a visit to the police officer, Clem Matherson, in his little office. "Have you heard anything that would be of any help to us?" Robert Graham asked, but Clem had not.

"I drove over to Hampton to speak to my boss about your jewels," he told them, "but he didn't have any advice to give. The first thing that any police officer would think of is that someone stole them and hid them in the well by an empty house, and was waiting for a chance to get them out of the neighborhood after the first search was over. But we haven't had any word of a jewel robbery anywhere. There hasn't come any notice for us to look out for someone suspected of such a thing. You may be sure we're watching, but we'll all just have to lie low and wait. The truth is bound to come out sooner or later. Jewels like those can't stay hid long."

It seemed that it was on the warmest morning of all that Nina went up the hill with Mrs. Gregory, with the hot wind blowing in their faces, to work at Kent's place. He himself was just going out with some letters to mail. He told Nina what needed to be done as he walked to the door. He must have worked most of the night, for the place was in even wilder disorder than usual. Nina noticed that he had set a row of bottles on the window sill, probably because the shelf below had got overcrowded.

As was now her habit, Nina first carried the jar of fish out to the kitchen to feed them and change the water. After that she took one armful of bowls and bottles to the kitchen sink and brought them back clean and shining. She was just gathering up another when suddenly an extra strong puff of wind came in at the window and toppled a big, heavy jar off the narrow sill. It fell crashing among the row of containers on the shelf below and they, in turn, went splintering to the floor. A fearful smell arose as the liquids ran together on the old, dry boards and in an instant a column of flame leaped up, with a cloud of strangling smoke that swept through the room.

8

A Promise

For a few seconds Nina stood without moving, watching the great wavering flame go up in the middle of the laboratory. She was a girl with a cool head and she did not, at first, feel too much fear, she was so busy trying to think what to do. She recollected once seeing her father spill some gasoline on the garage floor, how it caught fire, and how he snatched the robe out of the car and smothered the flame. She ran into the kitchen where she knew that there was a rug under the table. Mrs. Gregory was not much use. She screamed when she saw the burst of fire outside in the laboratory, and

she kept crying out, "What shall we do? What shall we do?" But she did help Nina move the table and try to drag the heavy rug to the door.

There was a pounding of feet on the stairs and Nina thought that it was Kent come back to help them, but instead it was Andrew Clark, Jeff, and Clyde on their way to Clyde's house. They each seized a corner of the rug and managed to pull it across the floor and over the fire. Mrs. Gregory, having got over her first panic, brought a bucket of water and began throwing it with a cup over the dry boards where the fire was spreading quickly. Under the rug the fire began to smother, throwing out thick clouds of choking smoke. They were all black with it; Nina's hair had been singed in front, and the room was a fearful confusion of water and smoke, shouting boys and crunching glass. Then they heard Kent coming up the steps two at a time.

"What is this?" he cried out at the head of the stairs. "Nina, what have you done? What have you done?" His voice was desperate.

The three boys had slid away, not because they were afraid of sharing any blame, but because they actually did not know at all what had happened. Nina knew that they were waiting below, until she could come down and tell them. She stood facing Kent, her hands full of papers which she had managed to gather up from the shelf where the bottles had fallen, scattered though they were.

Mrs. Gregory had vanished into the kitchen. She was, after all, a timid little old woman and she loved Kent too deeply to be able to endure his wrath, for wrath it was that was written on his face. Nina drew a long breath and spoke.

"That big glass thing in the window blew down. It broke a lot of other bottles and they all ran together and the fire spurted out." She said it clearly and almost calmly, and she put down the bunch of notes carefully on the table. Then all of a sudden she dropped down on the little stool by the kitchen door and burst into a torrent of tears. It would have been perfectly impossible for her to speak another word.

Kent stood silent, then came over to where she sat, with her face hidden in her hands. "Nina, Nina," he said, "can you ever forgive me for speaking to you like that? It was my own fault for leaving any such thing on the window sill. It was you, I know well enough, that got the fire put out. And you got my notes and records away, so they were safe. All my work would have gone for nothing if they had been burned. Oh, can you forgive me?"

Still she could not speak and he stood watching her for a minute, then leaned over her. "Nina, you are my friend, my good patient friend. Don't cry over what I said. I was wrong. Oh, my dear, don't cry!"

She got out a word or two then, though it was almost as difficult as though she had been

Clyde. "I'm—I'm not crying about myself or what you said. I'm c-crying about you."

"About me?" Kent echoed. "Why should you cry about me?"

"Because you're so unhappy," she sobbed. "Because you work so hard to forget how troubled you are. That's what Mrs. Gregory says. You won't come near us any more, even though you were lonely. It is all about those wicked jewels. I found them. I wish I never h-had."

Kent was quiet for so long that at last she ventured to look up at him. He was staring out of the window and the look on his face was one that she had never seen before, it was pure sorrow, as though he could never be comforted again. He drew up a chair at last and sat down beside her.

"It's quite true," he told her slowly, "that seeing the jewels there on your table upset me very much. But the sorrow I had been feeling was already there and I had been trying to run away from it. Yes. Mrs. Gregory is right, I have been trying to forget it by working harder and harder. I would explain the whole thing to you if I really knew the answer myself. But I don't. Nor do I know how to get the jewels back to their rightful owner, for I don't know where he is."

"But you know who he is?" Nina asked. She had stopped crying now.

"It's not hard to guess," he answered. "But the whole thing is a long story and you and your family would have to know the whole of it to understand. I'm so busy now, Nina, so pressed with this work that I'm trying to finish, I can't pull my wits together to think it all out about the jewels, and what to do with them. But once I'm free of what I'm doing, I will sit down and tell you all I know about them. That's a promise. Can you wait just a little longer?"

Yes, Nina thought, she could have patience to wonder and worry just a little longer. She gave him a wet smile and stood up. "I'll wait," she told him. "I'll have to go home now."

"Probably you will never want to help me again," Kent said and his voice was full of real regret.

"Oh no," she returned. "It won't be like that. I'll do anything I still can. I hope the fire and all the mess won't put your work back too much." She ran away down the stairs, far more light-hearted than she had thought she possibly could be after that dreadful moment when Kent came in.

If Andrew Clark had not made friends so quickly with the Grahams, he might have had a very lonely time at his brother's place. But as it was he seemed to enjoy coming every day to the Red House. The three of them always found something interesting to do. He taught Jeff to fish and Nina liked to go with them, to explore the reaches and pools of the brook and to look here and there for new birds and flowers. She came across a white wild orchid for the water garden. Barney said it was a real find and helped her plant it below the big willow tree.

Sometimes Clyde came with them, but not always, for his short legs grew tired before theirs did, and Nina would have to take him home. Andy stayed for meals many times at the Red House and, although he had been a little shy at first, the table was always a place of cheerful chatter when he was there. He was a little older than Nina and did not seem to feel himself in any way too old for Jeff. Although they were beginning to get acquainted in the village and might have found playmates there, here on Clark's Hill they found enough good company among themselves. Only Nina thought often of one playmate more.

The two dogs were always with them. Casey had grown, even since the Grahams had first met him. His legs were longer and, if possible, more awkward than before. But with his sharp-pricked ears, his shapely narrow head, and smooth black coat he already showed signs of growing up to be a beauty. He was fond of them all and sometimes did not seem to quite know which house was his real home. But he evidently felt that Clyde was more or less under his care and made unskillful efforts to see that nothing happened to him. He loved and admired Arthur greatly and, when they were all out together, followed at a clumsy gallop wherever the smaller and older dog went.

There had been a night of rain, not so violent a storm as had caught Nina on the Island Rock, but enough to raise the water of the brook and send it down cloudy with mud and stirred-up sand. Nina, Jeff, and Andrew went up the hillside to inspect the water garden and see whether any damage had been done. They found Barney Gates there before them, on the same errand. One or two of the bigger stones in the loose wall between the garden and the brook had shifted in their places and needed to be settled again. Barney had brought a bag of tools and was chipping away at the stones' faces to get them more closely into place. It took all four of them to accomplish this under Barney's directions, for the stones were large and the brook was full. The afternoon was well gone before they had finished, wet and muddy but properly proud of what they had been able to do. They had not been thinking of anything else, and it was Jeff who asked first, "Where are the dogs?"

No one, so they now realized, had seen them for the last hour. They called and Barney blew a piercing whistle on his fingers, but there was no resulting crashing among the bushes to announce their return. "Oh, they'll come back all right," Barney said easily. "Dogs are smart enough not to lose themselves the way people do." He took up his hammer and chisel to flatten the top of the last stone.

More time passed, with one or the other of them calling again and again, "Here, Arthur! Come, Casey!" but with no answer. The boys were for going farther down the stream to find a place to fish, but Nina insisted, "Don't go, don't go until we know where they are." Then, since she had very quick ears she lifted her head and said suddenly, "I hear something. I think I hear Casey yelping."

They all listened and in a moment a favoring puff of wind brought the sound again and they all heard it. And, bursting through the bushes came Arthur, whining, running about in circles, jumping up on each one in turn, dashing off into the woods from time to time and then coming back again. "There's something wrong with Casey, that's for sure," Barney said. He had just got the rock balanced and not quite in its place. "I can't let go of this job for a minute. You go on ahead and find him and I'll come after. There's no knowing what might have happened to the dog, the way he goes poking his nose into everything."

The three all ran after Arthur, who seemed greatly relieved and went charging through the woods. He took a straight line that was hard to follow for those who had only two legs and wore clothes that caught on briers and clutching branches. As they went on they could hear Casey's yelps sounding louder and louder. The way was steep and uphill. They could not keep up with

Arthur and kept having to call him back. He brought them, at last, to the foot of the wall of rock that rose straight up above their heads, as high as the roof of the Red House. Arthur ran to and fro, sniffing, and then, reaching the little trail they had followed earlier, began to scramble up. Jeff, who was a remarkable climber, went first, and Andrew followed, stopping now and then to give a hand to Nina.

They mounted, panting, and came out on the level above. There everything was the same, the stretch of grass, the big rock under which the mink family lived and the scattered boulders. And there was Casey at the edge of the grass, leaping and tugging at something that held him and crying out in loud, frightened puppy barks.

"He's got his foot in a trap," Andrew said, as Nina ran across to kneel down beside him. It was true, the dog's foot was held between the metal jaws of a trap that was chained to a big stone, so it could not be pulled away. The jaws were wrapped with heavy rags, so that whatever creature they caught would not be injured, but the fright of being held fast was sending the young dog into a perfect frenzy of desperate struggling. When Nina put her hand on him and spoke to him, he lay down, trembling and whining, quiet for a minute, and licked her hand. The two boys wrestled with the solid rusty jaws of the trap but could do nothing to pry them apart and presently Casey, taking fright again, began to pull and fight once more.

"If we could get the chain loose, at least he wouldn't pull so," Andrew said. "He'll end by hurting himself badly if he keeps this up, though he isn't hurt now, only frightened. Perhaps we can work the chain off the stone, it isn't fastened very tight."

It took desperate effort, pounding with stones, prying with sticks that broke under their hands, but little by little the rusty chain began to give way. "Bring him out so the chain lies straight," Andrew directed Nina, "and hold him quiet the best way you can."

Nina managed to move the frightened dog farther out on the grass, so that the chain pulled a little apart from the stone. Jeff had found a stouter stick, that, for once, did not crack into splinters with the first force upon it. Nina caught a hasty glimpse of the mink mother, peering out from under her big rock, and then disappearing in great haste. The chain scraped, moved a little, and slipped down toward the smaller end of the stone. "Now," Andrew cried, "hold the chain straight while we give a great heave. Here Jeff, both together! There, it's moving, it's coming. Now!"

The boys shouted, the chain gave a final harsh scraping noise and came free, and Casey gave one more desperate plunge. Nina, trying so hard

to keep him quiet had not thought at any time to look behind her to see how near they were getting to the edge of the rock. She was holding tight to the struggling dog when she stepped backward —into nothing. With her arms still around Casey they both went out and downward into empty air.

9

Night Ride

Nina could hear Barney's voice, though she felt dazed and it sounded rather far away. "If she hadn't had her arm around the dog, the trap would have broken his leg for sure," he was saying. "As it is I don't think there's much harm done to either of them. See if you can hold him still while I get this wrench at work on the trap." Casey had been so frightened by their sudden plunge over the rock that he lay very subdued and still while Barney worked at the stiff nuts that held the metal jaws.

"I thought it might be a trap he'd gotten into, so I brought my bag of tools. Somebody set it, looking to catch a mink, I expect, and it must have been left there since last winter. People don't trap in summertime, and it's against the law to set a trap and not look at it every day. When the fellow who set this took his traps in, he must have overlooked this one. These rags on the jaws are rotted but they've kept the dog from being hurt." There was creaking and scraping, as the wrench took hold, and a final clash of metal as the trap fell apart. Casey sprang up, almost stepping on Nina's face and rushed away, limping a little but evidently with no real hurt to the paw that had been caught. Arthur leaped and yelped about him, overjoyed to see his friend set at liberty again.

Barney Gates was bending over Nina now. "We had to get the dog free before we could get to you," he said. Nina's head was clearing. She tried to sit up but could not. When she tried again a hundred prickles and scratches told her that she was held fast in a heap of brier bushes. Barney had his garden shears out and was cutting and snipping all about her. "Just don't try to tear loose," he cautioned. "It's lucky the briers were here, nothing could have broken your fall better. Now, give me your hand."

She got up and stood unsteadily while Barney and the boys pulled the long clinging brier branches off her shirt and blue jeans. Barney had to do some more cutting to get them all out of her hair. It was true that the thorny bushes had done good service in catching the force of her fall.

Though she was dizzy for a minute or two, after a few steps everything around her steadied and she could walk without trouble. "It's all right," she assured them as they pressed round her. "And I'm so glad Casey isn't hurt."

Barney was gathering up his tools. "I don't want to see just that kind of thing happen again," he said. His voice was shaky, though Nina's was not. "I guess I won't work on the garden any more today. It's time we were all getting home."

Nina, after a bath and with antiseptic put all over the scratches on her face and arms and after throwing her ruined shirt and jeans into the rag bag, felt as though the adventure was fully and thoroughly over. The really important thing of the whole affair was that Casey was safe. They had all learned to love Casey, for he was an endearing dog with his puppy ways and his earnest, loving face.

Mrs. Gregory did not come for Nina next day so that, not unwillingly, she stayed quietly, in the windowseat, reading a book from the village library, for there are few villages in New England, no matter how small, that do not have a library. This one was at the edge of town; it had been a farmhouse once and they still stored hay in the shed at its far end. She was so absorbed that she jumped when she heard the telephone ring. It stood on the table in the big library room. She heard her father answer, "Yes, this is Robert Graham. A telegram you say?" The crackling voice in the receiver replied, taking some time, for it was evidently a long message, and when it had finished Professor Graham said sharply, "Read that again." It was some full minutes before he put the receiver down and came to the door to say to Nina, "Where's your mother?"

She jumped up, letting her book drop. "Don't be frightened," her father said, "I didn't mean to startle you, nothing has gone so very wrong, it's just something very pressing. But find your mother."

Jane Graham came hurrying in from the garden, summoned by Nina. "What is it?" she asked anxiously. Nina's father was gathering up pages of typewriting scattered all over his desk.

"The telegram is from Atkins, my publisher," he explained. "The arrangement was that they would have to see the first section before they could arrange to put it on this year's schedule. And I thought I had until the end of the month to get it ready. But I have made a mistake in the date; they need it at once. The telegram says that they hope the manuscript is on the way. The special editor who has to pass on it is going away and they must settle their plans, Atkins says, by the end of the week. That means Friday. And this is Wednesday."

"What happens if it is a day or two late?" Jane Graham asked.

"If it misses the special meeting before Howard goes, then it will not get on this year's list and will have to wait over for another season. Above all things I don't want that. I have this first part written, but I have to go over it and correct it. And I'm not a good enough typist to make the final copy for printing."

"Surely there must be somebody in the village who can type it for you," Nina's mother said.

"There must be," Robert Graham answered. "But it's a long job at best. We ought to find someone within the hour."

"I'll take the car and go down to ask all around," Jane Graham said. "Start on your correcting. I'll find someone. Nina, do you want to come with me?"

"I'll need her to help me," Nina's father said. "I want her to sit here beside me and number the pages as I pass them to her. To get them all together and the chapters in order is the first thing." Nina felt a little tingle to know that she could be of use.

They heard the car go out presently. Jeff and Andrew were off somewhere and the house was very quiet as Nina sat there by her father, counting the pages as they came, putting down the figures. The numbers mounted and mounted. Could anyone manage to get all this copied before tomorrow? She could hardly hope that anyone could and she wondered if her father thought it was impossible too. But he went on correcting and adding notes and she did not speak.

It was well after lunchtime when Jane Graham came in. She threw her hat down on the table and dropped dejectedly into a chair. "I couldn't find anyone—anywhere," she declared. There was despair in her voice. Her husband looked up, his forehead wrinkling with anxiety. "Not anyone, not anywhere?" he echoed.

"I asked in every possible place," Nina's mother said. "Durham has a great many things you wouldn't expect in such a small town, but it doesn't have enough typists to go around. All the ones that have jobs can't get time off. All the ones that know how are too busy putting up corn and tomato pickles, or canning peas or having a new baby. I went at last to George Sylvester at the bank—he's always so nice to me when I go in there—and he said he would telephone around and try his best to find somebody. He'll call up as soon as he gets a person that he thinks could do it. We'll just have to hope."

She went away to get lunch ready and Robert Graham went back to his work. But Nina saw that he was desperately worried. "It's all I'm going to be able to do to get the corrections made," he said. "I can't think about anything but that. It surely isn't true that there is nobody."

Nina's mother brought in lunch on a tray and Nina and her father ate as they worked. They did not talk at all. It got to be two o'clock in the afternoon, then three, and the telephone had not rung. "Would it be worth while to call him?" Jane Graham asked as she came in to take away the dishes, but Robert Graham said, "No, he'll surely call us. We can count on him."

It was half past three when a car came in from the road and drew up before the door. George Sylvester got out and came in. Nina jumped up and ran to meet him, for her mother was upstairs. "I didn't find anybody," he began and Nina thought she must burst into tears, but he added— "So I came myself."

"But it's for typewriting," Nina said aghast, "and there's such a lot of it." But George Sylvester only grinned and answered, "Don't you think that someone who began in the bank as an office boy might have learned typing on the way up. And I'm quick, too, because my old boss, Mr. McIntyre, used to roar at me if I wasn't. I'll just speak to your father and then go out and get my typewriter out of the car."

When Nina opened the door of the library and brought him in to her father, Robert Graham was as astonished as she had been. But he was quickly satisfied, he was in such dire need of help. "But see the amount of it that has to be copied," he said as he showed the pile of pages Nina had been numbering. George Sylvester was taking off his coat.

"I'm prepared to make a night of it," he returned. "You don't know how it has weighed on me that I turned you away that first day and this is a small chance to make up for it. You might perhaps know, Professor Graham, how proud Durham is to have a distinguished scholar like you living here in our community and have a book such as yours is bound to be, written right here in our midst at the Red House. Now, what paper do I use and where do I begin and how many copies?" In a moment his typewriter was installed and he was at work. Nina tiptoed out and met her mother at the door. Jane Graham did no more than peep in and then came back to go with Nina out into the garden and rejoice aloud. "How wonderfully good of him," she said.

The typewriter clicked steadily, sometimes with the sound of a second one along with it as Robert Graham had reason to revise a whole page. It is said that the editorial room in a newspaper office, when the paper goes to press is a place of great excitement, but it can well be matched by the scene in a writer's own house when the manuscript of a book gets off to the publisher. Discarded sheets of paper are thrown on the floor, wild searches are made for pages that have got mislaid, messengers go back and forth to fetch this and that at sudden need, and in the midst of all the confusion the pile of neat, clean beautiful final copy grows and grows.

The afternoon passed, it grew dark. Jane Graham and Nina brought in coffee and sandwiches again, the two workers said they could not eat anything else and were back at work the moment the last one was finished. Once or twice George Sylvester came out to walk rapidly up and down the porch to stretch his legs, but Professor Graham did not leave his place. When the boys came home Jane Graham gave them supper in the kitchen with warning not to make an unnecessary sound. They went out afterward, then finally Andrew went home and Jeff came in to bed. Nina was told that she must go to bed too, there was nothing more that she could do. It was wonderful, it was thrilling to think of a book coming into being right there in their own library, forming somehow from the rough pages she had sorted and numbered. "Are you going to bed too, Mother?" she asked.

"I'm just going to lie down on the couch and sleep a little," her mother answered. "I want to get up at midnight and make them coffee again."

Nina thought she could not even close her eyes, she was still so anxious over whether the copying could be finished in time or not. Though she left her door open in case she should hear anything going on that she might have part in, she nonetheless fell asleep quickly. She awoke finally in the pitch dark and hearing voices slipped into a shirt and jeans and went out to see how things were.

"It's three o'clock, Bob," George Sylvester was saying. It was plain that these two had been getting very well acquainted in the hours they had worked together. "You see how much is finished and less than the last quarter of the manuscript left. I'm going to be able to finish that easily by five. And you have got to the end of your part. When the thing is done it will have to be taken over to the airport to be mailed, to get there in time. You can't drive safely after being up all night, so go and get some sleep and trust me to get to the end." Even though he was unwilling, Robert Graham saw that this was reasonable and finally went away to bed. Nina peeped in on George Sylvester clicking away, he looked round at her and smiled but he did not stop even for a word.

She slept again and when she awoke it was still dark but there was moving about and talking in the next room. She ran out to see that George Sylvester had got up from the typewriter and was lighting a cigarette. "It's done," he said delightedly, "and time still for your father to read it over before he has to go." He pulled out a drawer to look for a big envelope to put the manuscript in. In the kitchen Jane Graham was frying bacon. Nina's father came in. He had slept and was now the widest awake of them all. To see one's own book setting out into the world is a good moment and not a breath of it should be wasted. "I'm no great scholar," George Sylvester was saying, "but you needn't think I don't know a magnificent piece of writing when I see it."

"It doesn't look like anything to me any more, I've worked on it so long," Robert Graham returned ruefully. "I'm doubting whether they'll see anything in it at all, there at Atkins's. But I'm certainly glad that we have the job finished."

Nina had a sudden thought. Her father had gulped a hasty breakfast, had dashed through the neat, careful pages of George's typing, had closed and sealed the big envelope and was now putting on his coat. "I want to go with you," she said. She was full of the same excitement as the others and wanted to see the affair through to the very end. Robert Graham looked questioningly at her mother.

"Why not?" Jane Graham said. "I hate to think of your going all that way alone. Get some breakfast eaten, Nina, while they do up the package."

In the library Robert Graham was handing the address label to his helper and she heard her father say, "Put it into your typewriter to write the address. I—I find my hand isn't as steady as it might be." What her father said in thanks to George Sylvester Nina could not hear, but they both came out smiling. That bad meeting on their first day in Durham was due to be thoroughly forgotten.

"You must be dreadfully tired," Jane Graham said to their friend but he answered, "Certainly not. It was much too exciting. And to see a fine book like that unfold under my hands was something that will probably never come my way again. There was once when Clem Matherson and I watched all night at the bank, after we had been warned that a gang was operating in our direction and we might be held up. That was the longest night I ever spent. If Barney Gates hadn't come in about midnight and kept us going with funny stories I don't know how we would ever have kept awake."

By this time Robert Graham had brought the car round and George Sylvester said that he would stay for a little while to help Mrs. Graham clear up but that the errand must not wait a minute. They all came out on the porch and found that there was a thin mist lying on the hillside and that the mountains opposite were not to be seen where usually they loomed up against the stars. "I hope it's clear down below," George Sylvester said as Nina climbed in beside her father and was given the precious package to hold. "You've just about time to make it. Well, good luck." They sped away down the hill.

But George Sylvester's wish was not to be fulfilled, for the fog grew thicker as they went down toward the valley. Robert Graham turned the lights up, but they thrust only blindly into the mist ahead. Nina could hardly tell where they were, even as they went down the familiar road. They were coming to the village, she knew, but there was nothing to be seen except here and there a prick of light where someone was getting up early. They had to go very slowly through the single street, but, once they were beyond the green, the car picked up speed again, though the fog was so thick that it was like a blanket hung just outside the windshield. Nina held her breath. What if they should meet another car, would they be able to see the lights in time to turn out? Or what if someone was crossing the road in the dark. But they must hurry, they had to hurry. What if their slow course at first had spoiled their whole chance? Once two dim blurs of light came out of the darkness, were suddenly blindingly bright as they went past and disappeared again. "Watch out at your side," her father said. "If you begin to see the weeds I'm too near the edge of the road." She kept her eyes glued to the shoulder; it was good to have something to do rather than just sit and worry. Once a tall stalk of goldenrod brushed their fender and she cried out in warning so that her father veered quickly toward the middle of the road. They were going up a long hill and she could feel, rather than see, when they were going down again. Then suddenly the mist was gone and they were in another valley. Far away down a long straight stretch of road they could see twinkling lights.

"It's the airport," Robert Graham said. "We'll just make it."

Nina, at last could make out the dim form of the waiting plane, with its great ghostly wings faintly visible in the gray light of the coming morning. They were turning in at the gate now, and suddenly the floodlight on the field went on, the plane was in full view with its own lights pricking out all over it. They reached the entrance of the airport building and stopped. "Stay with the car," Nina's father directed, seized the package, and ran in through the revolving door.

She knew that her father would have to stop at the little post-office window first, but would it be open? She could hear a throbbing noise, the plane was warming up. A big policeman came strolling by and stopped. "I think your dad parked in the wrong place," he said to Nina. "Could you call him back?"

"Oh," she cried. "He has to get a package on the plane. It's his book." Through the glass walls of the building she could see people getting into the plane, the last one went up the steps, the door closed. A man, yawning, was turning the steps to wheel them away. The policeman had disappeared.

10

Barney

Nina would never have thought that anyone so large as the policeman could have moved so fast. She saw him shoot out of the airport building, and heard him roar, "Hold it, there, bud." The man with the steps turned round in wonder and in an instant she saw her father rush out through the gate and go running across to the plane. The door opened again, a man leaned out and took the precious package. He smiled, nodded, and waved as he door slammed once more and Nina caught sight of a pretty stewardess smiling over his shoulder. The plane was moving and her father and the police-

man stood watching as it went taxiing down the runway, lifted to its toes and was no longer touching. In a moment more it was overhead, turning in a wide circle. She saw her father and the policeman gravely shaking hands.

They turned the car homeward in the gathering daylight, moving at a comfortable pace now. The fog had cleared completely and the straight length of road was empty ahead of them. Nina settled herself comfortably with her eyes on he great stretch of pink sky just above the horizon, vhere the sun would soon be up. Its red edge began o show and she glanced at her father to make sure hat he saw it too. As she looked, his head nodded orward. She seized his arm, "Daddy!" she cried, 'You're asleep."

He woke with a start. "Yes, I was dropping off he admitted. "I'm dead sleepy. I will just pull off the road for a bit and get it over with. I'm not fit to drive right now." He slid lower in his seat and closed his eyes. Some idea must have been going round and round in his mind and, as he slipped away into sleep, he said, "It's friendly people, isn't it, that make everything possible. Thank God for them!"

Nina sat by him, watching the sun come up. She had been much too excited to quiet down so soon, so she stayed broad awake as the time went by. The sun was up now, with long level rays creeping over the wide stretch of woods and meadows, the sky was bright blue overhead. At home her mother and Jeff would probably be sound asleep still. But Kent would be up and stirring; he would be going out to the laboratory to begin his day's work. She was not sure that she would be able to go up to help him today. She felt that once she got home sleep would rise up and drown her.

Her father moved presently and opened his eyes. He had not been asleep more than half an hour but it seemed to have been enough. He started the car and they went on through the glittering morning. They mounted the same long incline and went down once more into the Durham valley. Here wreaths of mist still stretched along where the little river ran, or clung to the lower slopes of the hills beyond. "There's a cloud sitting right on our house," Robert Graham said as he swung the car to the left to go up Clark's Hill. How familiar it was now, when only such a short time ago they had turned into that road for the first time. There was, indeed, fog around them again, wrapping them softly, all cool and white. They had to turn the lights on to make sure where they were and to go into their own driveway.

Nina and her father slept solidly through the whole morning, and the affairs of the Red House moved about on tiptoe to make sure that they would not be disturbed. Mrs. Gregory knocked gently at the kitchen door and nodded as Jane Graham explained in a whisper why Nina could not go with her. "Barney Gates told me she went with her father to the airport," Mrs. Gregory said. "He met George Sylvester going home before daylight. Barney stays late in the village sometimes. No—he doesn't drink, it's only talking."

It was high noon when Nina awoke, completely rested now and full of pleasant relief to know that the crisis of last night was safely over. When she dressed and came out of her room, she found that her father, too, was up and about. But he was not at work at the big table in the library as he had been day after day before. He was wandering about the living room, looking out of the window, evidently finding it difficult to settle down to anything. Her mother was in the kitchen preparing lunch. "As soon as we have eaten," Jane Graham said, "I'm going down to the village to thank George Sylvester again and to tell him the parcel got safely on the plane. Would you like to come too?"

"I think," Nina answered, "that I'll go up and see Mrs. Gregory. I want to know how things are at Kent's laboratory and see if anyone fed my guppies."

The morning mist was fully gone as she went up the road, and a brisk summer breeze was blowing cloud shadows across the mountain sides. Mrs. Gregory was in her little garden, tying up the grapevines that covered the trellis at the far end. Nina sat down on the little bench that was close beside her and began to ask her earnest questions about the laboratory.

"There's quite a pile of bowls and dishes waiting for you," Mrs. Gregory told her. "Kent wouldn't let me touch them. He was very polite about it, but he said you knew just how to handle them and that not many people did. And the guppies? When I came in this morning he was feeding them himself. And you may be surprised to know that there are all of a sudden about twice as many as you brought in from the brook. The new little ones are so tiny you can hardly see them."

They talked gaily there in the sunshine until suddenly there was an interruption. Barney Gates came in through the white gate. Nina could see at a glance that there was something wrong with him. It was not only that his cheery grin when he greeted people was faded to almost nothing. He had, somehow, a wilted look, as though all the good spirits had gone out of him. Even his shabby hat was no longer set at its old jaunty angle. He lost no time in telling Mrs. Gregory what was the matter.

"I met Kent up there in the driveway. He told me to give him back the keys of the big house, he was going to get somebody else to go in and keep it clean. He said I hadn't gone in there once, since—since the folks went away."

"And wasn't that true?" Mrs. Gregory asked briefly. "You know it was."

"Yes, it was true," Barney admitted "There's a good many times I meant to go up and do it, but it always seemed that it could wait. What was the use, I asked myself, to go there and sweep and dust and never anybody to as much as see it? I could do it proper, once I knew they were coming home."

"There's no way we are going to know when they are coming home—if they ever do," Amanda Gregory returned. "Mr. Charles gave me directions about the Red House. He said I was to go every week and see that it was looked after properly. Didn't he tell you what to do, that night before he left? And did you see him again in the morning?"

Barney explained heavily that "Mr. Charley" had sent for him suddenly in the middle of the night— "I had been late to the village so I was still up," he said. Mr. Charley had told him that he was leaving in the morning instead of the day after as he had planned. He gave Barney a letter to take to his brother George at once and give it into his own hand. "A strange time of night to be sent on such an errand," Barney said.

"And did you give it to him, as Mr. Charley told you?" Mrs. Gregory demanded.

Barney Gates hesitated, stuttered, but finally answered. "No—not exactly. It was all so dark and quiet when I got there that I didn't want to wake them. And besides, Mr. George was mad at me because I hadn't washed the car when he told me to. So I let myself in and put the letter on the hall table where Mr. George would find it in the morning."

"And was that the last you saw of Mr. Charley, the last thing he said to you?" Mrs. Gregory wanted to know. "He got me up early and asked me to bring down the birthday cake, and help him with some last things, though he had set out the table in the library all by himself. But in the end he went off in such a hurry he didn't even say good-by to me." That seemed to be something that had hurt her very deeply, for her voice shook a little. "Did he say good-by to you, Barney?"

"Well, as a matter of fact, he did," Barney answered. "He told me in the night there was going to be a party for the children around noon, and asked me to look in and see if everything was going well. He said the children liked me and that I could always pep up their parties." Barney's face had lighted as though this memory gave him some comfort. "And then later, he telephoned back, I expect it was from New York and asked was everything all right and did the party go off well."

"And what did you say?" Mrs. Gregory had dropped her pruning shears in the grass and had come to stand directly before him. They both seemed to have forgotten Nina's presence completely.

"Why," Barney was slow in bringing out his answer, "the truth was I had been up so late on his errands that I overslept next day and didn't get down there in time for the party. There was no one around when I went down."

"But what did you tell Mr. Charley?" Mrs. Gregory pushed the question.

"I—I didn't know what to say," Barney said. "It stood to reason that if he invited the three children to a party they must have come so I just said, yes, sure they came. And he asked again, did they have a good time, did they get their presents. I knew it was what he wanted to hear so I said again, "Sure, yes, everything was fine. Then he just said 'So long, Barney' and hung up."

Nina ran to Mrs. Gregory, who looked dizzy and as though she were going to fall. "You told him that?" The little old woman's voice was hardly more than a whisper. "You told him they came? Didn't you know that they never did?"

She turned to go into the house. "No, dear, don't help me. I'd rather go alone," she said to Nina and then she added, "Oh, what terrible trouble one lie can make!"

"It certainly wasn't a very big lie," Barney said as he and Nina stood looking at Amanda Gregory walking slowly up the path to her door. And he repeated, "I thought it was what he wanted to hear. I don't understand at all what this is about."

"I don't understand either," returned Nina. She felt more confused than ever about the whole matter. But she left Barney sitting mournfully on the bench and went away to the house to see what she could do for her good friend who had evidently received such a deep and bitter blow.

Mrs. Gregory was sitting in the big chair in the kitchen, openly weeping. She dried her eyes when Nina came in and tried to speak cheerfully. "You mustn't mind me, dear," she insisted. "It was just a shock to me to hear something I hadn't expected, I didn't mean to show that I was a little—little upset."

"I'm going to make you a cup of tea," Nina said, for she had seen her mother doing the same, more than once, for a friend who came to her in trouble. She was a little clumsy in making it over a strange fire, and she was fairly sure that Mrs. Gregory didn't really want to drink it. But the little old lady swallowed it dutifully and it did seem to make her feel somewhat better. She spoke much more steadily when she thanked Nina and said, trying to be very cheery again, "Now don't think about me any more. I'll be quite all right in a very little while. There's a basket of roses out there that I cut for your mother and set in the shade. You had better get them down to her before the sun wilts them."

There was nothing more that Nina could say or do, so she went out and gathered up the roses. Barney Gates was gone.

While her mother was arranging the flowers, Nina went over with her all that she had heard pass between Barney and Amanda Gregory. "I don't see quite how all that would have anything to do with us," Jane Graham said. "Of course in the end it must have something to do with the jewels, but how that explains how anyone could go away and leave jewels in a well, I don't see."

Nina was still going over it in her mind as she went back up the hill to return the basket to Mrs. Gregory. "I'm just as mixed up as ever," she concluded. "Oh dear, I wish Toots would come back and tell me all about it."

That evening Andrew Clark stayed for dinner, as he very often did. Afterward they sat around the living room table and Nina's mother read aloud out of *Treasure Island*. Andrew was very careful about getting back to his brother at the promised time and, absorbed as he was, he glanced more than once at the clock. At last, when Mrs. Graham paused at the end of a chapter, he got up. "It kills me to leave Jim in the apple barrel," he said. "But I don't want Kent to spend even a minute worrying or wondering where I am."

"Couldn't you give us just another hour," Jane Graham said. "It does seem too bad to leave the book just there."

"I would have to go up the hill and tell him I'll be an hour later," Andrew said doubtfully. "But if you really want to go on—"

"Sure we do," Jeff said, jumping up. "I'll go up with you. Keep Arthur here won't you?" The spaniel had cut his foot on a stone and they were all trying, not very successfully, to keep him quiet. Mrs. Graham suggested that Andy spend the night, but he declined.

"Kent might not even notice if I stayed away without telling him," Andrew said. "But I don't want that. I think he likes to have me there, even if he has no time to talk to me. I'm little enough good to him when he's working so hard."

Kent did stop for a minute to laugh and joke with them, but he had turned back to his work again almost before they started back down the stairs. "He says it won't be very long now before he is finished," Andrew said as the two boys went out of the door below. "But he won't really rest or get enough sleep until he comes to the end."

It was a dark evening and the big house loomed up against a cloudy sky where there were no stars.

They were not talking as they came near, along the grass-grown driveway; a long day of playing outdoors had made them a little quiet. Jeff was a trifle ahead and he stopped suddenly. "Andy," he said, "there's someone up there on the steps of the house beside the door." He spoke under his breath.

The boys stood still. Yes, it was true, there was a dark figure close to the big door, hardly to be seen in the shadows. As they both watched, the person moved a little, but evidently did not see them. It was a man who seemed to be trying to peer inside through the narrow window beside the door. He tried one view and then another, as though he could not see. Jeff drew a quick breath and then stepped back, for he was a little frightened.

"Should we go back and tell Kent?" Jeff asked.

"I don't know," Andy answered. He did not want to disturb his brother unless he must. They stood in doubt for a moment and then Andrew said firmly, "It doesn't look as though he were trying to break in. I'm just going to walk up and see who it is."

He took a step forward and Jeff felt he could not do anything but follow him.

11

Four Days

The two boys had delayed a little too long, for the dark figure in the doorway moved suddenly, then turned and ran nimbly along the porch and jumped into the bed of roses beyond. They could hear him crashing through a hedge and then running down the hill beyond the garden. There was no use in going after him, they decided quickly. They went on down the driveway, walking rather close together and it was with something of a sigh of relief that they went up the steps of the Red House. Nina was watching for them from the door.

"Did you see anyone go by?" Jeff asked breathlessly. No, she had not, except for Barney Gates who had walked past on the road. "He seemed to be in a hurry so I didn't speak to him," she said.

"It would be hard on Barney if he didn't get down to the village in the evening to talk to his friends," Andrew observed. "He's worked around the place for a long time, but, with all the family away, he has let himself down. He was supposed to clean the big house now and then, but he hasn't gone near it. One day when Kent was able to pay attention he told Barney not to come back and took the keys away from him. It made Barney feel bad but it was what he deserved. Now let's get back to the apple barrel."

No one could help noticing how nervous Robert Graham was during the next few days, and how his mind seemed to be on anything but what was going on around him. He would forget about meals and have to be summoned; he would go on errands to the village and come back without what he went to fetch. He covered up his typewriter, saying, "What's the use of my going on when I don't know whether Atkins will even care to print what I've been trying to do. They'll probably send the whole thing back and I'll have had all my trouble for nothing."

Nina was very much distressed to hear him talking so. She did not know that nearly all writers feel the same way while they are waiting for a publisher's judgment, feeling more anxious about the result the harder they have worked to accomplish it. "Why don't I hear from them?" was another thing he kept saying. "I'm not going to write another word until I have their opinion." Nina, however, had seen him looking through his papers and scribbling notes as though he would like very much to begin work again, but had no heart for it while he was still in his miserable uncertainty.

It was on one of the mornings when he was especially discouraged and restless that Nina's mother persuaded him to come for a walk with her down through the woods to the orchard. Nina had volunteered to do the breakfast dishes alone, so she did not go with them. They had been gone perhaps half an hour when she heard the telephone ringing in the library. She sat down in her father's chair to answer it. "This is Western Union," said a voice. "A message from New York for Professor Robert Graham. Is he there?"

"No," Nina told him, "Professor Graham is out."

"Then will you take it down as I read it?" Western Union said.

She reached for a pencil, and in that instant a thought went through her like a sword. This was surely from the publishers! Perhaps her father was right after all, that they did not like the book and this was a message to reject it. And she would have to take the telegram to him!

Western Union was reading in a sing-song voice.

"Manuscript of book received and read. Congratulate you on a magnificent piece of work. Best thing you have ever done. Are publishing it at early date. Letter follows. Atkins."

Nina had put it all down in her careful, square writing, but when she finished she asked to have it read again. She was sure that she had heard correctly but she wanted to hear the joyful news once more. Yes, it was just as she had written it. "We will mail you a copy of it," Western Union said politely. "Thank you."

She sat for a minute, drinking in the solid delight that good news brings. Then she sprang up and ran out. She must find her father and mother quickly. She went running through the garden gate, down what was now a path. Once it had been merely the line that her feet and Jeff's had taken when they came that way on the treasure hunt. Mrs. Wren was singing on her perch on the porch behind her as she went. Back through the woods she ran until she found the brook and then down along it until she came out into the orchard, her feet flying. She could see her father and mother sitting on a log by the biggest apple tree. They were not talking for evidently her father was too worried to pay attention. Oh, how good it was that she could be the first to bring the good news! She came panting up and laid the message on his knee.

As he read it Nina saw a slow smile spread over his well loved face. He handed it to her mother without a word and when she had finished it he read it again. "I put everything I had into the book," he said. "It's good to know that somebody saw something in it after all." He smiled at Nina. "I think the Red House that you found has brought us luck," he said. "Now I can go on with a good heart." He got up quickly. He seemed to feel that he must hurry home and begin work at once.

Cheerfulness flooded the Red House again, and the typewriter keys fairly danced under Robert Graham's energetic fingers. Days passed and the pile of pages mounted. Only the first section had been written, and there was a long road still to go

to get to the end of the book, yet there was no doubt in anyone's mind that all would go happily now. But there were two undertakings yet to be carried out. One was Kent's work in the laboratory. The other was the finding of the owner of the jewels. And both of them depended on Kent.

Often at night Nina would wake to think of the two brothers there on the hill above. Was Andrew sleeping, she wondered, or was he awake and listening to Kent going back and forth in the shadowy laboratory? Was the great experiment, as Andrew had said, so near the end? Would it mean that Kent would get his scholarship and go back to college? Or might something have gone wrong? She would drift off to sleep and wake to wonder again.

It was one early morning, near dawn, when she woke suddenly to hear a sound outside. It seemed to her that she had heard the chugging of Kent's little car through her sleep, and now she heard his voice. "Nina," he was saying softly. "Nina, are you awake?"

She slipped out of bed and went to the door of her parents' room. Her mother heard her and came quickly to ask in a whisper what was the matter.

"Kent is outside," Nina told her. "He wants to come in."

Kent it was indeed, his hair tousled, his hastily put on jacket buttoned two buttons wrong. But in spite of this look of weariness, his face was bright with happiness and relief. "If you don't mind," he said, without any apology for waking them, "I want to use your telephone. I tried Barney's house, but his door was locked and he sleeps so soundly I couldn't get in. I have to call my professor at the university. He told me to let him know the very minute I finished. I think that what he gave me to do has turned out to be something much bigger than we ever thought. He will want to know right away, I am certain."

He went into the library and they closed the door after him. They could hear him indistinctly inside, his voice high-pitched and quick with excitement. The person at the other end seemed just as excited. At last when Kent spoke more slowly and perhaps a little louder, they could not help overhearing. "Yes, Dr. Craig, I will write you all about it and send you the notes, but not for a few days. There is something else I have to do, something very important that can't wait any longer. It will take four days."

He came out of the library. Mrs. Graham had gone into the kitchen to make him some coffee. "You've really finished?" Nina said, and the next words burst from her. "You promised that, when you were done, you would tell us—"

He stopped her. "I know what I promised," he answered. "But I'm going to do better still. I don't really understand the whole thing about the jewels myself, but I think I know now who put them into the well and why. Right now I don't know where he is, but I'm going to find him and bring him back to put some very wrong things right. We owe it to your family. You should have the whole story so that you can really understand. So I'm going to go and get my Cousin Charley to tell you himself. There's an office in New York that can get me in touch with him, and there's that early flight from the airport that I just have time to make. I ought to be back in four days. Could you take Andy in while I'm away?"

Nina nodded. She knew that her father and mother would want to. When her mother came in a few minutes later with coffee on a tray, Nina told her, "Kent is gone." All he had taken time for, Nina had noticed, was to put right the two buttons on his jacket.

Four days seemed very long to wait but they passed somehow. Jeff and Andrew enjoyed each other's company and did not seem to get impatient. But for Nina the time crawled by, as Barney Gates had said, "like a wet week." When the fourth day came at last she woke in the morning with the one thought that now the time was here. Will it be this morning or this afternoon? she wondered, when he—when they—will get here? For he was to bring someone with him.

There was somebody else who had also been finding it hard to wait. In the middle of that morning a gray-haired gentleman appeared at the door of the Red House and asked at once, "Has Kent

Clark got back? I am Dr. Craig, his professor at the university. I have been most anxious to see what he has to show me."

Nina took him in to her father. As Kent had said, they knew each other. "My daughter can take you up to the laboratory," Robert Graham said. "She knows more about what is up there than I do."

Professor Craig looked as though he did not quite believe it, but when they got to Kent's working place and she got out his notes and records, he sat down quite satisfied. "The one thing I used to find fault with him about," he said, "was the wild disorder in which he kept any place where he was working. I did manage to teach him that his records had to be legible and in order." Dr. Craig pulled up his chair to the desk and got out his glasses. "But it looks as though someone had managed to do some straightening up here. It always seemed to me as though, if he were left to go his own way, Kent was bound to have an accident some time."

Nina was silent. She thought that Professor Craig should hear about the fire from Kent himself. How fortunate it was that none of the precious records had been burned. She went about the room, putting unimportant things into their places until she was sure the professor had everything he wanted.

"It isn't usual for anyone of your age to be so good a helper," he observed at last, looking at her over his spectacles. "Are you going to our university when you are older and will you study with me? Are you planning to be a chemist like Kent?"

"No, sir," she explained. "I think I want to work with things that are alive—and that don't go off if they get mixed together. But I am going to study at Highgate; it's my father's university, your university, and Kent's. I'm making an experiment now, a guppy experiment. Since I have so many I put them into two jars and am feeding them different food to see which set grows the fastest."

Back at home she tried to settle down with a book. Somehow she would have to get through the rest of the day. Jeff was sent up to invite Dr. Craig to lunch but he sent back word that Mrs. Gregory was there and would attend to his needs so that he could eat while he read. The afternoon crept away. It was evening, it was getting dark. "He said four days," Nina kept repeating to herself. Surely he would not disappoint her. At least he would send her some word if he were not coming. A big round moon rose over the mountains opposite. "It's bedtime, Nina," her mother said at last. Nina made one final effort.

"Couldn't I just walk down the driveway to the road and see if he isn't coming up the hill?" she begged.

"I think you might in this bright moonlight," her mother agreed. "I'll wait here on the steps and watch you go. But be quick."

It is true that Nina was not exactly quick as she walked down the driveway, though she tried to make herself be. But as she got nearer the gap in the wall she heard the sound of an automobile, the chug, chug that had to be Kent's little car. She stood still to wait until he came round the curve of the driveway. She heard the car stop and then, to her surprise and dismay, heard it go on again up the hillside road. What could it mean? She was sure that it was Kent. She ran forward and saw somebody coming in, someone not very big, a little bigger than herself, with bright hair in the moonlight.

"It's Toots," she cried out, and ran to meet her.

12

Promise Fulfilled

The two girls hugged each other there in the moonlight, as though they had been friends all their lives. "I'm so glad you've come," Nina said. "I've waited so long."

"Kent talked about you all the way along the road," the other girl answered. "And with all he told me I could hardly wait. We're all coming home. My father had to stop for some business along the way, so Kent and I came on ahead. He's gone up to get Mrs. Gregory and have her fix up the house a little before the others get here. But I didn't want to wait even for that, so he put me off here at your gate. Now tell me all about everything.

Are my guppies all right? Budge and I ran down to put them in the water that night before we left. Kent told me that you found them in the little pool."

The two sat down on a big stone by the driveway and began talking a hundred words to the minute, about the guppies, about the Island Rock—"I was there in a rainstorm once too," Toots said. "It was a good while ago and my doll slid over the edge and went whirling down into the deep pool. My daddy came to get me. And do the quail still whistle in the deep grass in the orchard? It seems a dreadfully long time since we went away."

Jane Graham, waiting on the steps, finally came down the driveway to see what all this was about. "It's Toots," Nina announced joyfully and that seemed to be enough explanation for the moment.

"And can Toots tell us about the jewels and whose they are?" Nina's mother asked. Nina looked up, startled. In the excitement of seeing Toots she had not yet got to asking questions about the jewels.

"I just couldn't quite tell you," Toots answered. "I don't really know, myself, whose they are. We've talked and talked about it, but I don't understand yet. That's what we have all come home for. Kent said it was the only thing to do, to get together and have everyone tell what happened, the Grahams and all, so we could get it straight. He was sure it was the only way. He talked about the Grahams all the time and he said we would all like you. Here's Kent now."

The little car came down the road and into the drive. Mrs. Gregory sat on the back seat, all smiles, such smiles as Nina had never seen on her kind old face before. Things are beginning to be right, Nina thought, if she can look so happy already. Toots climbed in and gave her a great hug, then got on the front seat with Kent.

"The others ought to be along in about two hours," he told them. "We're going to try to get things a little cleaned up before then. The place must be smothered in dust."

"We'll come up at once to help you," Mrs. Graham answered promptly. "Go on and we'll come after with some buckets and brooms. I'll bring the vacuum cleaner." Kent nodded his pleasure and thanks and the car moved on.

He went out of sight and Nina and her mother turned to go toward the house when they heard the sound of feet coming down the road. Heavy feet they were but, just the same, moving so fast as to be almost running. Barney Gates came into view, puffing a little from his great haste. Yet he paused for a moment to speak to them.

"If anyone asks for me, anyone at all," he said, "tell them that I've gone to visit my cousin over in Hampton. I've been meaning to for quite a while and this—this seems to be a good time to do it. I can get down to the village just in time for the bus if I hurry." He looked as if he were about to run again.

"But you mustn't go!" Nina exclaimed. "They're all coming home, all the Clarks. And they don't know what really happened that time Mr.—Mr. Charley went away and telephoned back to you. You've got to tell them."

"That I won't," returned Barney fiercely. "I didn't do much of anything wrong and I meant it right. I won't talk to nobody about it." He turned to go, but Nina followed him begging.

"Please, Barney, please," she insisted. "It's important, I know. It's terribly important. They came home to find out."

He only shook his head obstinately and hastened his long strides as he went away down the hill. "There's no use in following him," Mrs. Graham said, "I don't see at all what he has to do with it, but certainly you can't stop him."

Nina came back, disappointed and anxious. But it was true, Barney Gates was running away and it seemed as though the whole puzzle was still to be left untangled. "I wish he had waited," she lamented.

With Robert Graham at the wheel they all got into the Graham car, taking Andrew with them, while the two dogs followed behind. The big house was no longer dark above them as they came up the drive. Every window was lighted and the wide front door stood open. Mrs. Gregory was already at work with Toots helping her, but Kent was standing by the table with a letter in his hand. "I found this lying on the table, covered with dust, when I came in," he said, his voice puzzled. "It's Charley's writing and it has his brother's name on it." He was putting it into his pocket when Nina suddenly remembered.

"Professor Craig is here," she told Kent. "He came this morning and he said he couldn't wait to see what you had done. He's at the laboratory now, didn't Mrs. Gregory tell you—"

Kent didn't give her time to finish. He bolted out of the door and went running up the driveway. Mrs. Gregory had not heard, she must have been far too excited over Kent's news to remember anything about chemistry professors. "I expect he's forgotten about us by now," Toots said cheerily. "Well, the others will be here pretty soon."

They made good progress among all of them, and inside of two hours the great rooms downstairs were made quite themselves again. It was a beautiful house with big fireplaces, a wide winding stair, and an immense kitchen where Mrs. Gregory was making coffee. "It was lucky that Kent knew how to turn on the electricity," she said. "We had to go outside into the garden to get water."

Then, with all of them there—the four Grahams, Andrew, Mrs. Gregory, and Toots, a big car drove up to the steps, a car that seemed to be full and overflowing with people. Nina was sitting down for a minute after a whirlwind of work, when a tall young man stepped in. Except for his black hair and dancing black eyes, he looked something like Kent. He looked about him for a moment, dazzled by the bright lights in the wide hall. Casey fell upon him with cries and whimpers of delight. "Down, Casey," the young man said and looking up, questioned, "You're Nina? You saved my dog when he was in the trap. That by itself is enough to make me grateful to you always." He turned about and he and Toots began making introductions as the others came in. The black-haired young man was Charles Clark himself; he was the Mr. Charley who had lived in the Red House and was Toots's uncle. The other man was his brother George, shorter and not so handsome; he was Toots's father. And this was her mother, Mrs. George Clark, small and pretty. And these were Highlo, a slim girl almost grown up, and Budge, square and solid and older than Andrew. Everybody hugged Mrs. Gregory in delighted greeting, though she kept saying, "Now, now, Mr. Charley," or, "There, Budge, you're going to be the death of me."

In the midst of all the tumult of talk, several voices asked, "Where's Kent?" for he seemed to show no sign of returning.

Robert Graham said, "I think we need him as much as Dr. Craig does. Nina, suppose you and I walk up to fetch him. Toots is right—he has probably forgotten all about us."

They went out into the cool moonlight and saw that lights were ablaze all over the laboratory. As they mounted the narrow stairs, they heard Kent's voice, excited and happy, going steadily on and on explaining. "I finished all the others before I came back to this one, Professor Craig." Nina and her father came in and the two men sitting with their heads together, broke off their talk, and looked up.

"A highly satisfactory piece of work," Dr. Craig said to Robert Graham, and his smiling eyes told her that he was saying it to Nina also. "What Kent has found will be of the greatest help to me. I know I mustn't keep him, you need him for your family council. Since you were good enough to ask me to spend the night at your house, Dr. Graham, I'll come down to you later but I'll stay here to look through a few more of his records. By the way, I am hoping to have him for a special laboratory assistant next winter."

It seemed as though Kent were going to make some excuse for staying longer, but when he put his hand into his pocket for a paper to write a memorandum his face suddenly changed. "I carried a letter away by mistake," he said, a little ruefully. "I'll have to take it back, but I must talk to you later, Professor Craig. I have so much to tell you."

Professor Craig nodded, his eyes already going down a new page. Nina noticed that it had a little scorched mark on its edge. Had Kent told him about the fire, she wondered.

There was a great sound of chatter and laughter coming out of the open door of the big house as they came up the steps. It dropped as Kent came in. "I shouldn't have dashed away like that," he admitted apologetically. "Hearing that Professor Craig was here made me forget everything else. But I did remember to bring back this letter." He took from his pocket the envelope that he had found on the table and gave it to Toots's father. George Clark looked at it bewildered. "How in the world did this get here?" he asked. But no one could answer.

Robert Graham spoke in the midst of the little wondering silence that followed. "This," he said, "is a good old-fashioned town where the bank stays open on Friday evenings. And I am determined that before I sleep this night, the jewels are going out of my possession and into their owner's. Will you go down with me?" he said to Charles Clark who answered, "Why, yes," but then added not very helpfully, "Yet I don't consider that they are mine."

But Kent intervened. "I believe that, first of all, we ought to sit down and get this whole matter cleared up. It won't take long, if each person just tells what he knows. We still will have time to get to the bank and someone can go down to the Red House and telephone George Sylvester to wait until we come. He'd be glad to."

They all agreed and presently they were sitting

in a wide circle around the great empty fireplace at the end of the hall. Toots was on the arm of her father's chair and Nina was sitting close beside her. Charles Clark brought a chair for Mrs. Gregory. She did not want to sit down with them, but in the end she did. There was suddenly a silence that no one seemed to want to break.

It was Charles Clark who finally began. "The Graham family has the right to know all of it," he said, "after what they have done for us. It's not easy to tell, but I'll make a try and I'll get some help from George." He looked across at his brother, who nodded.

The story came out, not all in one piece but clear enough as far as it went. The two Clark brothers had inherited from their father the two houses, the Red House where Charles lived alone, the big house for George and his family. And there was something more. The elder Mr. Clark, where other rich men collected pictures or rare books, had collected jewels over a long stretch of years. It grew in time to be a famous collection. He had left it to his two sons to be shared between them when Charles was twenty-five.

It was on the night before Charles's birthday that the two brothers sat down, in the library of the Red House, to arrange the division. They were all planning to go away within a day or two, George and his family to drive to Florida and Charley to go abroad on scientific business for the government. But over the division of the jewels they quarreled, quarreled bitterly and terribly, as two hot-tempered brothers, even though they love each other, can sometimes do.

"It was the first time it had happened since we were grown up," Charles Clark said. "And it was just the way Mrs. Gregory said it would be, that it didn't seem to mean much when we were boys, but that it would be very different when we were grown men. We each had a different opinion and neither of us would give in."

Charles, it seemed, was not especially interested in the value and size of the jewels, but in the rarity and beauty of some of them, and had thought, at first inspection, that those which his brother wanted him to have did not make a just share. Such hard words passed between them, one word leading to another, that in the end George flung himself out of the house, leaving on the table what he thought was Charley's proper half. In his anger he had made up his mind that he would never speak to his brother again, that he could not even live as his neighbor any more. When he got home, even though it was nearly midnight, he wakened his family, and said that he had decided to start off at once. They were all packed and ready to go; they had sometimes traveled at night before, to escape traffic, and so they went without asking too many questions. They could not know that George Clark, in his heart, meant never to come back.

They drove out by a different entrance to the place and Charles did not hear them go.

It was Charley who had the quickest temper, but who usually got over his anger first. He knew, inside of an hour, what harm had been done between them. He decided that, if the jewels could cause such trouble, he did not want any part in them, and he thought they ought all to be in a single family anyway. He wrote a letter to his brother, saying that if George would make up the quarrel, he would also. He invited them all to come to his house next day, to celebrate his birthday and to take part in a treasure hunt and he gave a very plain hint as to what the treasure would be.

He could not make up his mind even yet to go himself to make peace; he was not sure of how he would be received. So he telephoned Barney Gates and sent him up with the letter, saying that it must be delivered into George's own hand. He hoped that George might come down at once, even though it was so late, to say that the quarrel was at an end. He waited an hour, two hours, and there was no word. He decided then that he could not face George, and that he would leave at once instead of a day or two later as he had intended, and would take the early plane from the airport. He got up at dawn to spread the clues that the children were to follow. He was purposely quiet when he slipped up to the big house and slid the first one under the door, and was naturally not surprised that the house should be so silent at that hour of the morning. He fetched Mrs. Gregory and she brought the cake she had ready for his birthday. Since he had already planned some sort of a party for his birthday and had brought the favors and ornaments for the table, he had set most of them out himself before she came. And he had already hidden the jewels in the well bucket, knowing that it was never used now, and feeling sure that they would be there for only a few hours.

"That's as far as I can go," Charles said. "There's a piece of the story missing somewhere, I don't understand what happened next." Nina and Mrs. Gregory looked across at each other. Would they have to tell what Barney Gates had said to them? It would be a hard thing indeed to do so.

But they were spared. Somebody was walking, walking slowly and heavily, up the drive and there was a knock at the door, a hesitating tap at first, then a firmer one, a knock by someone who knew that he could not afford to wait. Barney Gates came in. His usually ruddy face was pale now, his cheery smile quite gone. He did not allow them any time for questions.

"The little lady here told me I ought to wait and explain things, but I told her I wouldn't do it. It was true—I was running away. But something wouldn't let me. I got down to the village and stood there and watched the bus go without me, and then my feet just turned me around and marched me up the hill again. So I have come back. I had to tell you."

He told again what Nina had heard him say to Mrs. Gregory, how he had gone up to the big house with the letter, and found it dark and silent, but did not know that it was empty. Instead of trying to put Charles's letter into his brother's hand—"Mr. George was mad at me"—he repeated, "I just left it on the table." And when Charles had telephoned back, to ask about the party, and did the children get their presents, he had not wanted to admit that he had overslept, and just answered "Yes, yes," to all his questions. "After Amanda Gregory told me that they never came, I went up in the night to see if the letter was still there. I thought I could see if it was."

George Clark took out of his pocket the letter Kent had found and given him. So much had been happening that he had not yet read it, but he tore it open and his eyes went down the page as everybody watched, waiting. He finished, looked across at his brother Charles, nodded, and smiled. It was the end of the quarrel. Now everything was plain.

Kent, knowing that something was very wrong between the brothers, could not bear to go into the empty house, so the letter had lain there all these months. And Charley, being told by Barney that his gift had been received and having no word concerning it, had been too proud and hurt to ask anything further.

"And I hated the jewels by that time," he said. "When Kent came to fetch me, I still refused to go home or to see the others. But when he told me how the Grahams had found the jewels, how they had given up their other plans and settled down to find who owned them, why, like Barney here, I had to come." He looked at the disconsolate Barney, still standing near the door. "You're not fired any more, Barney," he said. "The Clark family can't do without you."

Robert Graham was looking at his watch. "We've just time to get to the bank," he said. Charles and George Clark were going with him.

Jane Graham raised her voice a little above the chatter of excited talk that had broken out. "I want to know this: Has the Clark family had any dinner?" It seemed that they had not, and that no one had thought of it until that moment. "Then we will look for you all at the Red House in about three quarters of an hour," she said, and added to her husband, "I'm coming to the village with you, Robert. It is good that Durham has shops open on Friday night."

Nina and Toots, whispering together in a corner, had a wonderful idea. They slipped over to whisper to Mrs. Gregory and she beamed and nodded. "Kent," said Toots, "get your car. We have an errand for you too."

So it came about that when the Clarks and the Grahams gathered a little later at the Red House, they found, spread out on the table in the library, the same sort of feast that Charles had got ready so many months ago. Besides the barbecued chicken and the other smoking good things that Jane Graham had supplied, there were the flowers, the little animals, the place cards and the snapping crackers. And there in the middle was the heap of jewels, winking and glittering in the light of the candles in the tall candlesticks. There, finally, was Mrs. Gregory, carrying in the same cake, blazing now, and everyone, from Professor Craig down to little Clyde, wearing paper caps was standing up to sing "Happy Birthday."

Charles Clark, at the head of the table, rose to offer his thanks. "It is true that it is a little past the proper time, but it is a happy birthday indeed, the happiest I've ever had. The presents go elsewhere, for my brother and I are going to give the collection to the Metropolitan Museum, where they really belong. Three of the more modest settings go to Highlo and Budge and Toots. We wanted to give some to Nina but her parents would not allow us. We are celebrating my birthday, but I am sure that you will all agree that Nina, with Jeff to help her, are the ones to cut the cake."

Kent, who had said very little through the whole evening, came to hand her the knife. His face was shining with happiness.

"Blow out all the candles," he said. "But I don't think we have anything left to wish for."